PRAISE FOR CAROLINE LINDEN

Praise for *At the Christmas Wedding*

"Perfect seasonal fare – warm, light-hearted and perfectly romantic, laced with humour, filled with likeable principals and served up with a soupçon of Yuletide cheer and festive frolic."
—All About Romance

Praise for *Map of a Lady's Heart*

"A truly warm and romantic tale."
—Roses are Blue

MAP OF A LADY'S HEART

CAROLINE LINDEN

CAROLINE LINDEN

PROLOGUE

KINGSTAG CASTLE

DECEMBER 1816

A storm was coming.

Viola Cavendish didn't need to look at the sky to know it. She could recognize the signs, all of them ominous, converging upon Kingstag Castle. Even worse, she had a very bad feeling she might find herself at the middle of it.

"I'm sure everything will be fine," said the Duchess of Wessex as she buttoned her fur-trimmed pelisse. The footmen were carrying down the duke's and duchess's traveling trunks, and the coach was outside the door. Viola could see the horses' breath steaming in the cold air as they stood waiting to carry her employers away for at least a fortnight.

The duke and duchess weren't supposed to leave for another month. The duchess's sister, Mrs. Blair, was expecting her first child after Christmas, and everyone at Kingstag could talk of nothing else. Well—all the females at Kingstag

1

were keenly interested in the baby, although Kingstag was mostly populated by females. Aside from the duchess, the castle held the duke's mother, the dowager duchess; the duke's three younger sisters, Serena, Alexandra, and Bridget; and an elderly relation, Lady Sophronia. Since Mr. Blair was a cousin to the Cavendish family, everyone felt some claim upon the child, but especially the duchess, who was eagerly anticipating the visit she planned to make when the child was born.

But yesterday an express letter had arrived from Mr. Blair, saying his wife's labor pains had begun almost a month earlier than expected, and she was begging for the duchess to come as soon as possible. The duchess and her sister were extraordinarily close; without hesitation the duchess declared that she was leaving at once. The duke argued with her— Viola had been ordered from the room, which was rare—but in the end the duchess had prevailed, although only on the condition that the duke would go with her.

That was the moment Viola foresaw the coming storm. As the duchess's personal secretary, she was privy to almost everything that went on in the castle, and there was quite a bit going on at present. Not only was it nearing Christmas, but houseguests were expected, and the dowager duchess was ill. With neither the duke nor the duchess in residence, the position of hostess would fall on Lady Serena, who was young and unaccustomed to presiding. The next ranking lady would be Lady Sophronia, but no one would dare leave her in charge. Lady Sophronia delighted in chaos and mischief , and she always claimed to be pining for a scandal.

Viola could smile at that when she believed the duchess or dowager duchess would be around to prevent anything untoward. Now, though, the dowager duchess was confined to bed with a cold, the duchess was leaving, and Viola had the horrible thought that *she* would end up responsible for whatever disaster ensued.

Not that she could ever express that thought aloud. Her job was to be confident and capable, no matter what was asked of her. That was why the duchess had hired her, and Viola wasn't careless enough to let something like a house party unsettle her—at least not visibly. She gave a poised smile in response to the duchess's assurance that all would be well. "Of course, Your Grace."

"The dowager duchess will surely be on her feet again in a day or two," her employer went on. "Serena's friends are delightful young ladies and I'm sure they'll be no trouble." She paused. "You might have to keep a close eye on Bridget."

Viola fought back a laugh. Bridget was the duke's youngest sister, and could be charitably described as high-spirited. Most of the trouble in the castle could be traced to Bridget.

On the other hand, Viola genuinely liked the girl. Once she had been just as enthusiastic and eager for adventure as Bridget was. Still, she said a quick prayer that Bridget wouldn't go looking for extra adventure and mayhem in the next fortnight.

"Be sure to send the tenants' Christmas baskets by the end of the week," the duchess went on, "and let Serena tend to the decorating; I've already discussed it with Mrs. Hughes and she can assist."

"Yes, madam."

"I expect Serena and her friends will be rather quiet." Worry shadowed the duchess's eyes for a moment. "If they wish to have some entertainment, allow it. Especially . . . Well, encourage it as best you can."

"Yes, madam." Viola understood the concern. Serena was the eldest of the duke's sisters, a charming beauty at age twenty-one. Until several weeks ago she'd been engaged to marry the Duke of Frye, pink-cheeked with happiness and excitement, and then one day the engagement was abruptly over, and no one spoke of why. Even Viola had no idea what had happened. Serena turned pale and silent, and her mother, the dowager duchess, had almost immediately announced a Christmas house party of friends to cheer her.

A burst of noise made both women look up. The duke was coming down the stairs, his secretary close behind. Because of the sudden change in plans, Geoffrey Martin was accompanying the duke, which left Viola even more in charge of the castle. Geoffrey was carrying the large traveling desk that contained the duke's correspondence, and he went directly out to the waiting coach and horses.

The duke came to his wife's side. "Are you ready, my love?"

"Nearly," she told him. "We're leaving poor Viola in a horrible situation, Gareth."

Wessex glanced at her. Viola stood a little straighter under his piercing dark gaze, and bobbed a curtsey. "I'll do my best, Your Grace."

"And that's why I'm not worried," said the duchess firmly, putting her hand on Viola's arm. "I have great faith in you."

"Thank you, Your Grace," she said with another tiny curtsey. Viola tamped down her sense of impending disaster, which was surely just her imagination. The duchess had hired her for her competence, giving her a home and an income when she desperately needed both. It wasn't only her own well-being that depended on it; her younger brother Stephen needed her support until he was old enough to manage it for himself. Viola would be forever grateful to the Duchess of Wessex for giving her such a plum position.

For the past two years she had devoted herself to earning the duchess's trust, and she wasn't about to lose it now. "I shall be guided by Her Grace the dowager duchess in every uncertainty."

"Quite right." The duke gave her a small smile, which did wonders to his face. He appeared very somber and intimidating until he smiled. "We must go, Cleo, if we're to reach Morland today."

The worry in his wife's face deepened. "Yes, I'll be right there." She drew Viola aside as the butler stepped forward with the duke's coat and hat. "Send someone to Morland Park if there's any trouble," she said quietly, naming the Blair home. "It's only ten miles, we can return in a day."

"Your Grace," protested Viola, "I'm sure that won't be necessary—"

The duchess made a subtle shushing motion. "Perhaps not, but if anything untoward happens . . ." Her eyes bored into Viola's, as if trying to convey something too terrible to say out loud. Startled, Viola could only wet her lips and nod.

"Very good." The duchess blew out a breath. "I hope all will be well, both here and at Morland."

"Yes, Your Grace. I dearly hope Mrs. Blair is well." Viola bowed her head. If Mrs. Blair's child was born too early, he might not survive.

The other woman smiled wistfully. "I wish we were taking you with us. I don't know what I shall do without you." She sighed. "I wish we didn't need to go at all yet."

The duke approached with her cloak. "We must go, Cleo," he said again. The duchess nodded, and Wessex folded the cloak tenderly around her shoulders.

Viola followed as they went out to the coach. Footmen rushed before them with hot bricks for the carriage floor. Geoffrey, his muffler pulled up almost to his hat brim, swung into the saddle of a gray gelding. The horses shook their traces as the duke and duchess climbed into the carriage.

"Good-bye," called the duchess, waving as a footman closed the door. The duke touched the brim of his hat, and the coachman lifted the whip and started the horses.

Viola waved back, hunching her shoulders against the cold. Running footsteps sounded behind her, and then Bridget Cavendish was beside her, swinging one arm exuberantly in the air. "Good-bye," she cried. "Give our love to Blair and to Helen!" The carriage rolled on, past the oaks.

Bridget lowered her arm. "I hope Helen has the baby safely."

"Yes," said Viola softly. "I hope so too."

"With Cleo there, I'm sure she will." Bridget turned to her, and Viola finally focused on her long enough to see the gleam in her eyes. *Oh no.* "Cousin Viola . . ."

"No," said Viola immediately. Her late husband had been one of Bridget's distant cousins, and Viola was therefore only a relation by marriage, but when the girl called her "cousin," Viola had learned to be wary of what came next.

"You didn't even hear my idea!" Bridget looked wounded. "It's not rude or dangerous. I'm sure Cleo would allow it, if she were here."

"And yet I can't help but note you did not ask before she left." Viola shook her head with a soft *tsk.* "What is it?"

Bridget brightened right out of her pretend hurt. "A play. To cheer Serena. It will be silly and make no sense at all and she'll be so diverted. Please say we may put it on!"

That didn't sound so dreadful . . . and yet it was Bridget, so Viola wasn't reassured. "Which play?"

"Oh, I'm writing it," was the cheerful reply. "Completely original. Nothing vulgar or inappropriate, I promise."

For a moment she was shocked into silence. It wasn't that Bridget wasn't bright enough or creative enough to write a play, it was that Viola had never seen her sit still long enough to write a scene, let alone multiple acts. "How exciting," she said, recovering. "May I read it?"

"Even better—you'll be in it!" Bridget's eyes glowed as she beamed back. "Everyone will be, except Mama if she's going to be ill for a while, and Great-Aunt Sophronia. They'll be our audience."

Her heart settled into a normal rhythm again. If Bridget meant for her to have a part, she'd have to see the play, and could put a stop to any nonsense before it got out of hand. And if anyone could make Serena smile again, it would be Bridget. For all her madcap ways, the girl was irrepressible in her good humor and wit, with a knack for making people laugh even in their foulest tempers. And the duchess *had* said to encourage entertainments.

"It sounds like a fine idea," she told Bridget.

"Thank you!" The girl clapped her hands and ran back into the house before Viola could say anything more, which was likely for the best.

A gust of wind made her shiver. She wrapped her arms around herself and cast one last look down the long oak-lined avenue; the ducal carriage was already gone from sight. Her gaze drifted upward. The clouds seemed to be growing thicker and grayer by the moment, and the air had a leaden stillness that promised snow.

Viola didn't like storms.

CHAPTER 1

"*How* much farther is it?"

Wesley Morane, Earl of Winterton, inhaled slowly and then exhaled even more slowly. If he didn't know better, he would think his nephew was still a child instead of a young man nearing his twenty-first birthday. "A few more miles, I expect."

Justin scowled and slumped by the window. The weak light caught his fair hair and made him look as young and petulant as he was behaving. "Aren't we nearly to Cornwall yet?"

It felt as though they had circled the globe in this carriage. Wes tried to keep his voice calm as he replied, "No." He did not repeat an earlier mistake, of offering to show Justin their progress on the small but handsome leather-bound atlas of England he kept in the traveling chaise. That had not gone well, with Justin fixating on the distance left to travel instead of the beauty of the illustrated map of Dorset.

Several minutes of silence passed. Wes did not fool himself they would continue indefinitely. Time had already seemed to stretch and slow, much like the distance they had still to travel. At one point he wondered if the carriage and horses had become stuck in a vast mud slick, where the hooves and wheels were only churning in place, never making an inch of progress.

"I could have stayed in Hampshire," Justin said abruptly. "Dorset is hideous in winter."

So is Hampshire. Wes managed to keep himself from saying it aloud. He did not manage to keep from thinking about a few places that were not hideous in winter—the East Indies, for example. The winter of 1808 had been splendid there, sitting under thick palm fronds and learning about the spice trade from his father.

"I recall you agitating to leave Hampshire," he said instead. "Your mother told me you were wild to be away."

The boy's mouth pulled sullenly. "Not this far away."

That was what his mother had feared. Anne was Wes's oldest sister, and she knew exactly what her son wanted, so newly grown to manhood and so abruptly possessed of his father's title. Justin had barely finished university when his father died, leaving him the new Viscount Newton. Instead of the Grand Tour he had been promised upon completing his studies, Justin had gone home to New Cross House to console his mother and sisters and lay his father to rest.

But mourning soon grew tiresome for a young man of high spirits and energy. If he couldn't sow his wild oats in Italy or Spain, Justin was determined to sow them somewhere. He fell in with a crowd of young dandies who spent their time racing carriages, dicing, and drinking at the local pub. When the local miller called on Anne to complain of young Lord Newton's attentions to his daughter, Anne wrote to Wes and commanded him to take charge of his nephew before the boy was hopelessly debauched.

He'd gone at once; he had to. Anne might be a decade older than he, but he was still the head of the family. Privately he didn't think Justin was in as bad a way as Anne claimed, but his sister was grieving her husband, and rationality had never been her strong suit anyway. It seemed obvious to Wes that the best course was to separate the restless son and anxious mother.

On impulse he decided Justin should come with him to Kingstag Castle in Dorset. Wes had his eye on a particular old atlas, and he strongly suspected the duke had recently acquired it. The only way to be certain was to see it himself, and his sister's demand that he deal with his nephew provided all the excuse Wes needed to set off for Dorset at once. Not only would it give Anne a respite from worrying about Justin, he reasoned, it would remove the boy from the miller's daughter as well as his wastrel friends for a fortnight, and allow Wes a chance to influence his nephew for the better.

Rarely had he regretted anything more.

"Where did you want to go?" he asked, wondering what had made him think he could act as a mentor to this sulking young man. Had he been this odious when his own father died?

"Italy," said Justin at once. "Rome. My father promised me I would see all the sights."

"That's an even longer journey," Wes pointed out. "Some of it aboard ships, which can be even more beastly than the roads."

"At least the destination is worthwhile," flung back his nephew. "I've nothing to do with the duke—"

"And you can only be civil and cordial to someone you've known for ages?" Wes raised one brow. "You've got a lot in common with Wessex, you know. He also inherited young. You might find him an interesting acquaintance."

The expression on Justin's face was just shy of incredulous. "I doubt it. He's old enough to be my father."

Not quite; Wessex was only a few years older than Wes, if memory served. "Your father would be pleased for you to know him," he said instead.

Justin did not reply. He turned to gaze moodily out the window again. After a few minutes, Wes drew out his travel atlas. He smoothed open the pages and his irritation subsided. The illustrations were remarkable, and he was able to locate their location to within a few miles. The travel guide provided plenty of description of the surrounding country-side, and he lost himself in vignettes of Roman ruins and splendid castles and manors.

"It's snowing," Justin muttered.

Wes turned a page, still reading about the stone circle found not far from here. "We're almost there."

"What if we have to stop and become snowed in at some dreary little inn on the side of the road?"

"I doubt that will happen."

Justin was quiet for a moment, then burst out, "We'll be trapped at Kingstag, won't we?"

Wes glanced out the window. It was indeed snowing, but not hard. "It's not likely, this far south. We're not in Russia."

"Might as well be," was the grumbled retort.

"You have no idea what Russia is like."

"Nor am I ever likely to!"

Wes closed the book with a snap. "Your behavior is the reason," he warned. "This is why your mother wanted you to come with me—I daresay she was sick to death of listening to you complain." He glared at his nephew. "If you wish to be treated as a man of sense, worthy of respect, you might begin acting the part."

Justin gaped at him. "I didn't ask for my father to die!"

"Neither did I," Wes retorted. "I was only five years older than you when my father died. Don't imagine I've forgotten what it was like." He softened his voice as Justin's eyes grew round and his lower lip jutted out. "Life serves us all some hard turns. Carousing at the pub and chasing the miller's daughter isn't something you are owed, and either one can cause long-lasting regret. Do you want to cause your mother even more anguish, on top of her sorrow at your father's death?" Justin jerked his head *no*. "I should hope not." With that stern pronouncement, Wes sat back and opened his book again.

For the next hour Justin said nothing. Once or twice Wes stole a glance at him under pretext of checking the weather, but Justin was simply staring out the window, shoulders hunched. He hoped his nephew managed to comport himself graciously at Kingstag. Wes didn't know Wessex personally, and his mission would be greatly complicated by a surly nephew. If Justin behaved like a moody child and cost Wes a chance to get that atlas . . . He breathed deeply and assured himself that would not happen; he would not allow it to happen. One way or another he would rein in Justin.

Finally the carriage slowed to turn into a winding oak-lined avenue. Wes put the book aside for good; it had grown too dark to read anyway, even with the lamps lit. Outside the window, one of the outriders galloped past on his way to announce them at the house. "I believe we've arrived."

Justin nodded.

"I recognize this is not how you planned to spend your holiday," he went on, trying to be understanding. "A viscount will be subject to duty and obligation, and not all of it is exceedingly pleasant. However, you can make anything as bearable, or as horrible, as you choose by how you approach the matter. Conduct yourself with grace and good will, and you will find yourself master of the situation instead of a victim gnashing his teeth over the gross indignity of everything."

"What am I do to here, Uncle Winterton?" asked Justin plaintively. "I know nothing about atlases or old books. I've never met the duke. It's the middle of winter and I shall miss Christmas with my mother and sisters. It feels like punishment."

"We'll be back in Hampshire by Twelfth Night. If all goes

very well, perhaps sooner. And I don't view it as punishment —a change of scene, nothing more." He waited, but Justin merely heaved a silent sigh. He accepted his fate, but without understanding. "Buck up, lad," said Wes bracingly. "When you were a child, you used to beg to come along on my travels."

"The East Indies sounded a great deal more exciting and exotic than Dorset in winter."

Wes laughed. The carriage had reached the front of the house, which was indeed a castle, though one shorn of moat and outer wall. "True enough! But you never know where adventure may be lurking." The footman opened the door, and Wes stepped out.

Justin followed, pulling his greatcoat tightly around him as he peered up at the massive stone walls of Kingstag Castle, doubt written on his face. "In Dorset? I can't imagine."

"Try." He strode forward through the swirling snow. An inch or two had accumulated, suggesting it had been snowing for some time here. With a sharp jangle of harness, the carriage started off again; the coachman would want to get the horses out of the cold as soon as possible. The butler was waiting in the wide open doorway of the house, holding a lantern aloft like a beacon.

The cavernous hall inside was dim, the candlelight no match for the soaring vaulted ceiling above. A footman pulled the tall doors shut with a clang behind them, while another servant took their hats and coats, and a third instantly stepped forward with a broom to whisk away the snow that had blown in with them. The butler bowed. "Good evening, my lords. Won't you come this way?" He led them into a cozy parlor nearby. A fire burned in the hearth, and Wes went to warm his hands, grateful for the heat.

"Are you certain they're expecting us today?" Justin lingered by the door.

Wes turned to let the fire warm his backside. "Why?"

His nephew shrugged. "It didn't seem as though they were." He drifted into the room, fiddling with his watch chain.

Time passed. More time passed. Justin began openly checking his watch, in silent demonstration that he'd been right and this visit was indeed a punishment. Wes grew restive. He had an invitation, damn it, from the duke himself. He had more or less begged for it—perhaps even almost invited himself—but he was still an invited guest. Today had been explicitly fixed as the date he would arrive, and however reluctantly the duke had agreed, he *had* agreed to that. Wes had roamed across half the world, and he knew how to plan and execute a trip on time, with minimal delays. Had it really thrown the duke's household in uproar, or was something more serious going on?

His fingers were reaching for the cord to summon a servant when the door opened at last. A woman stepped into the room—a very attractive woman, with toffee-brown hair and soft green eyes. His hand dropped back to his side in surprise.

"Lord Winterton," she said, dipping a curtsey until her dark blue skirts pooled around her. She raised her head and looked him in the eye with a warm smile on her lovely face, and Wes would have sworn the floor rose and fell under his feet like a ship on the sea in a squall. "I apologize that you've been left waiting."

His eyes fixed on her, Wes bowed. "Were we? I hardly noticed." Justin made a quiet noise behind him, and he started. He'd forgotten his nephew was in the room. "My nephew, Viscount Newton," he said, motioning toward the young man.

She made another graceful curtsey. It made her bosom plump up beautifully. "Welcome to Kingstag, Lord Newton."

"Thank you, ma'am." Justin's voice sounded deeper and more interested, which perversely annoyed Wes. This woman was too old for his nephew. Not that she was old by any stretch. In fact she looked to be just about perfect. But when he shot a glance of veiled rebuke at Justin, the boy was gazing attentively at the newcomer.

She came forward, her skirts swaying attractively. "I am Mrs. Cavendish, private secretary to the Duchess of Wessex. I'm afraid I bring unfortunate news. His Grace is not in residence now."

It took a moment for the words to penetrate Wes's brain. His attention had snagged on the way her lips shaped the words. "We had an appointment," he said.

She bowed her head. "I apologize, my lord. His Grace was called away rather abruptly. I believed Mr. Martin to have written to anyone expected, requesting a postponement."

"There's a snowstorm," protested Justin. "The roads are a nightmare."

Her face blanked for a split second, then turned pink. It was entrancing, and completely distracted Wes from the urge to correct Justin's rude statement. "Oh no," she said, her lips curving into a rueful smile. "I didn't mean you must leave, certainly not in this weather. You are very welcome to stay. I regret that I cannot tell you when the duke may return, though."

If someone had told him an hour ago that the duke would be away and his trip would be for naught, Wes would have snarled in frustration. Now, he stared at Mrs. Cavendish's smile and forgot all about atlases and the long carriage ride and the snow. "That is very kind. I hope Wessex wasn't called away on a tragic matter."

Her expression flickered for a moment. "Nothing of the sort. Her Grace the dowager duchess bade me welcome you, and convey her regret that she's unwell and unable to receive you herself."

Wes bowed his head and murmured a wish for the duchess's health. Both the duke and the duchess were away on urgent business—there could be no other kind that required them to leave in such weather—and the dowager duchess was confined to her bed. There must have been quite a search to find someone to tell him the bad news.

As it happened, he was not sorry Mrs. Cavendish had been the one chosen.

"Withers is having rooms prepared for you," Mrs. Cavendish went on. "May I send for some refreshment? You must be chilled and tired after your journey. The family dines in an hour, if you would care to join them."

"Thank you." Wes shook himself out of his daze. He was dumbstruck by a secretary; what a fine example to set for his nephew. Hypocritical, too, after warning Justin away from the miller's pretty daughter.

The door opened behind her before she could reply. A young woman, about Justin's age, slipped in. "Viola, may we —?" She stopped short at the sight of the two men, her mouth hanging open. "Are you a friend of Frye?" she asked Justin suspiciously.

Justin blinked. "Who?"

"The Duke of Frye," said the young woman with a trace of disgust, earning her a dismayed glance from Mrs. Cavendish. "The scoundrel."

A deep blush suffused his face. "N-No." He sucked in a quick breath and added, somewhat boastfully, "I am Lord Newton."

She brightened. "Oh! Are you joining the house party? You didn't tell me anyone else was coming, Viola."

Mrs. Cavendish put up one hand. "Lady Bridget, please." She turned back toward Wes. "Lord Winterton, Lord Newton, may I present Lady Bridget Cavendish, His Grace's youngest sister. Lady Bridget, the Earl of Winterton and Viscount Newton."

"A pleasure to meet you," said Lady Bridget cheerfully as she curtseyed. Her attention immediately swung back to Mrs.

Cavendish. "We need a ladder, loads of white feathers, and something that could portray a ghost—a tablecloth, perhaps."

"What? Why?" asked the other woman in some alarm, before she held up her hand again. "Never mind. We shall discuss it later."

Lady Bridget rolled her eyes. "But—"

"Later," repeated Mrs. Cavendish with a small shooing motion of her hand. Reluctantly, Lady Bridget went.

"I beg your pardon," said Wes. "I'd no idea there was a house party."

Mrs. Cavendish shook her head, but with a betraying flush on her cheeks. "It's only a few guests—friends of Lady Serena, the duke's sister. I shall urge them to stay out of your way. The castle is quite large enough for all."

There was really no choice. Night was falling, as was the snow. "Thank you," he said again, revising his plan. Perhaps it wasn't the worst thing to have an extra day or two without the duke at home. He could examine the atlas at leisure, to be sure it was the one he wanted. If not, he could take his leave and go without a fuss; he would say he needed to return Justin to his family in time for Christmas celebrations, as his nephew wished.

But if it *were* the atlas he wanted . . . This could be an invaluable chance to plan his strategy. The duke had not wanted to sell it, and had only agreed to let him look at it when Wes pushed all boundaries of politeness. It would take some persuading to get Wessex to part with the atlas, and any insight he could glean before the duke arrived home might prove vital. And he suspected the lovely secretary would know her employer's mind . . .

Yes, it suited him quite well to have missed the duke.

"We would be delighted to dine with the family," he said. "In an hour, you say?"

"Yes. Withers will send a man to attend you, if you've not brought your own . . . ?"

Wes shook his head. He'd got used to doing for himself on short journeys, and Justin didn't have a valet to bring.

Mrs. Cavendish excused herself and left. Wes turned to his nephew. "Well, that's quite a turn."

"What?" Justin was staring at the closed door, and flinched at his remark.

"That Wessex isn't here." Justin looked blank. "You shall get your wish to be home with your sisters for Christmas."

"Oh. Yes." The young man cleared his throat. "The house party may prove diverting."

Wes glanced at him with sudden suspicion. "Oh?" He could almost hear his sister's voice in his ear, urging him to deliver a lecture about proper behavior toward young ladies. Wes quieted it for the moment. Lady Bridget seemed full of high spirits, but the dowager duchess, who must be Lady Bridget's mother, was in residence. He wanted to be a mentor to Justin, not a nagging conscience.

And of course, he'd had a few improper thoughts about Mrs. Cavendish himself. If he scolded Justin for being mesmerized by a pretty female, he'd be the biggest hypocrite in Britain. He said nothing.

But when the butler appeared soon afterward to conduct them to their rooms, things took another turn for the worse. They hadn't even made it across the hall before a patter of footsteps and a rustle of skirts heralded the arrival of not one, not two, but four young ladies, including the mischievous Lady Bridget at the rear.

"Lord Winterton," said one of them, who seemed to be the leader from the way she stepped forward. Tall and slim, she was striking rather than beautiful, with very dark eyes and hair, but fair skin. "Lord Newton. Welcome to Kingstag Castle." As one, all four of them curtseyed, and Wes and Justin bowed. "I am Lady Alexandra Cavendish. My cousin Viola tells me you are here to see my brother Wessex, who has been called away."

"Yes," Wes replied. "We shan't intrude."

"Oh no." Her gaze moved to Justin, who seemed to be holding himself unusually erect, his chest puffed out a little. "We would be delighted to have you join our party. We're putting on a play, you see, and haven't enough gentlemen to fill all the parts."

"A capital idea," said Justin before Wes could speak. "Thank you, Lady Alexandra, we would be honored."

She smiled. "Excellent. Bridget will assign you lines." She curtseyed again. "Until dinner, my lords."

Justin stared as they left in a troop. Lady Alexandra glanced over her shoulder once to smile at him. Wes took one look at his nephew's face, and began shaking his head. "We're leaving tomorrow." He'd have to come back later in pursuit of the atlas. Making the trip twice was far preferable to spending his time watching Justin like a hawk. The last thing he needed was a scandal between his nephew and one of Wessex's sisters. The duke would never sell him the atlas then.

"No!" Justin grabbed his arm. "Please not, Uncle." He cleared his throat. "And, er, I just gave my word to be in the play."

"You've no idea what the play is."

"Does it matter?"

Wes ran one hand over his face. Four very pretty young ladies, without enough gentlemen to fill all the parts. His sister, Justin's mother, would be calling for the carriage—for the sleigh, if necessary—immediately.

But. On the other hand, the young ladies were obviously well-born. Wes would have to keep a close eye on his nephew, but perhaps this would motivate Justin to improve his manners. The Newton viscountcy made him an eligible match, after all, even if his sullen behavior did not. It might be a good lesson for the boy to see what sort of behavior appealed to decent young ladies.

And then Mrs. Cavendish's face flashed through his mind.

Cousin Viola, Lady Alexandra called her. Not merely a secretary after all. She seemed to be in charge of the place. Staying for a few days would probably thrust him together with her, as the only adults supervising this play . . .

"Very well," he said. "We can stay."

CHAPTER 2

$\mathcal{V}$iola personally took the dowager duchess's dinner to her on a tray. The duchess had been sick in bed for a few days now, but still insisted every evening she would be on her feet in the morning. Tonight Viola said a fervent prayer that it was true this time.

"Good evening, Your Grace." She set the tray on the table near the bed.

"Thank you, Viola." The duchess's voice was hoarse from coughing.

"Some visitors arrived today." Viola tidied the tray and uncovered the dishes. "The Earl of Winterton and his nephew, Viscount Newton. Lord Winterton had an appointment with the duke."

"Oh dear." The dowager coughed, and Viola handed her a cup of steaming tea. "Wessex will not be pleased to have missed him."

Nor was Viola especially pleased to have two more guests to entertain. "I thought Mr. Martin would have written to cancel their visit, but they must have set out before his letter reached them."

The duchess made a sound of dismay. "How regrettable."

Viola brought the tray over to the bed. The dowager was propped up on a number of pillows, looking older than usual. Her face was pale except for the flush of fever in her cheeks, and her eyes looked sunken and glassy. She'd fallen ill several days earlier and seemed to be in the worst of it. "Ma'am, perhaps we should send for the doctor—"

The duchess gave her a wan smile. "So says Ellen," she murmured, referring to her maid. "I've seen what doctors do, you know. I prefer to take my chances with the fever."

Viola frowned in worry. "Yes, ma'am, but . . ."

The duchess pushed herself a little more upright and pulled the tray toward her. "I have no plans to succumb to it, mind you. If I go into a decline and hope begins to wane, you and Ellen may send for the doctor, but as long as I have my appetite and can sleep, I intend to brave it out." She inspected the tray and sighed. "More blancmange. Tell Cook I would like something with flavor next time."

"Yes, ma'am." Viola hesitated. "What ought I to do with Lords Winterton and Newton?"

The duchess blinked. "Oh yes. I suppose they must stay the night."

She wet her lips. "It's snowing, Your Grace, and it shows no signs of stopping. The roads may not be fit for travel tomorrow."

"Then they must stay until the roads are fit." The duchess gave her a reproving glance. "You didn't think otherwise, surely?"

Viola blushed. She'd already told the gentlemen they were welcome to stay. "No, no. I only worried about the inconvenience to Lady Serena and her friends."

Something of the older woman's usual perception returned. "Are these gentlemen by any chance handsome, rakish fellows?"

"Rakish! Oh my, I've no idea," Viola babbled. "But . . . Lord Newton is rather young—near Lady Alexandra's age, I would suppose—and he is a handsome gentleman."

"Oh dear." Another fit of coughing seized the duchess, and Viola hurried to fetch a clean handkerchief. "And Winterton?" rasped the duchess a moment later, reaching for her tea. "Tell me he's a somber older gentleman capable of keeping his nephew in check."

"Er." Viola shifted her weight, picturing the man in question. "I wouldn't call him *much* older . . ."

The duchess closed her eyes and leaned back against the pillows. "Is there a Lady Winterton? Send Ellen to fetch *Debrett's*, Viola."

Viola rang for the maid, who returned a short time later with the tome listing all the aristocracy of Britain. She paged through it to the Earl of Winterton's entry and read it aloud to the duchess. "Wesley Edward Fitzallen Morane, Earl of Winterton, Viscount Desmond, Baron Lyle; born August 31, 1784; succeeded his father, Allen, the late earl, on March 12, 1810."

"No countess," said the duchess on a sigh. "And he's handsome." Viola opened her mouth to protest that she'd never said that, realized it was true, and said nothing. The earl was a man who drew the eye—at least her eye—with coal-black hair and vivid blue eyes in a lean, tanned face. He looked like a man of bold action and passionate interests.

"I shall have to recover." The dowager ruined this determined statement with another bout of coughing, and Viola refilled her teacup without waiting for permission. "There is no way Serena can maintain order. Even if these two gentlemen arrived as the very souls of dignity and propriety, Sophronia would corrupt them into the biggest scoundrels in England within a week. I shall be out of this bed by morning if I must be carried on a litter to do it."

Viola took one look at the dowager duchess, pale and weak and still feverish, and knew there was no way she would be recovered by the morning. "You mustn't risk your health, ma'am." She took a deep breath and girded herself. "I shall do everything I can to assist Lady Serena, and I'm sure we can manage between the two of us."

"Are you?" The dowager held up one hand to forestall a protest Viola wasn't making. "I know my daughters. Bridget, in particular, can be . . . willful."

Viola knew that all too well. This play of Bridget's was beginning to worry her; despite asking twice, she had yet to see a single page of it, and Bridget's odd requests were growing alarming. A ghost? Feathers? She said a silent prayer that she wasn't about to make a promise she couldn't keep, which might well lead to the duchess dismissing her from her post, and gave a decisive nod. "Of course. I'm very fond of Lady Bridget, and I'm confident I can guide her."

"Well," said the dowager, her voice heavy with doubt, "perhaps . . ."

"There's little choice, I fear," Viola added. "The roads will soon be impassable." She'd checked on the snowfall right before bringing the dowager's tray. The snow was four inches deep and still falling heavily. John the footman reported that Hugh, the head gardener, was predicting a great deal of snow, based on his observations of the squirrels at Kingstag Castle. Hugh claimed he could predict the weather by the animals' behavior. Viola wasn't convinced of that, but given the way her luck had run the last few years, this storm would be an epic blizzard that brought all of Dorset to a standstill.

The house was full of young ladies and gentlemen, with more expected, who would grow bored and restive if trapped inside for days on end.

Not one but two additional handsome gentlemen had arrived on the scene, soon to be trapped in that same house.

The duke, who could deal with the visiting gentlemen, was away and not expected to return soon.

The duchess, who could organize activities to keep the young ladies occupied, was also away.

The dowager duchess, who could maintain order and decorum by sheer force of will, was confined to bed for several more days at least.

Lady Serena, nominally the hostess in her mother's stead, could hardly be expected to supervise the friends who had been invited to cheer her after her recent heartbreak.

And that meant Lady Sophronia, who loved chaos and scandal more than she loved breath, would be in charge.

Viola recognized that she was the only person at Kingstag with any hope of preventing both chaos and scandal. She had expected that the duchess's absence would offer her a bit of a reprieve from work, when she might have some time for herself. With no small amount of regret, she realized that instead of enjoying some cozy afternoons by the fire with a good book or writing letters, she would be keeping a keen eye on Lady Bridget's play rehearsals, as well as on all the guests, especially the young ladies. Her heart sank at the futility of that endeavor. Perhaps she ought to keep her eyes on the gentlemen . . .

Then she blushed, thinking of keeping an eye on Lord Winterton. That wouldn't be a hardship. Keeping her eyes *off* him would be harder. But he didn't look like the sort to cause trouble with young ladies barely half his age—if anything, Viola thought the young ladies would be causing trouble over him.

Lord Newton, though, had gazed at Bridget with such interest, and Viola sighed.

"With luck the snow will be gone in a few days, and the gentlemen can be on their way—presuming His Grace hasn't returned by then, that is. In the meantime, I'm sure there will be no trouble. I shall keep a keen eye on the whole party."

The dowager still looked doubtful, but also relieved. "If you are confident you can maintain order, then I see no cause for alarm."

"I can," she promised the duchess with more confidence than she felt. "I give my word."

A servant directed Wes to a large formal drawing room before dinner. He hadn't seen Justin since shortly after they arrived, but he heard his nephew's laugh as he approached the drawing room doors. Since he hadn't heard Justin sound that happy in months, Wes's step quickened in a mixture of interest and alarm. What could have pleased him so much?

The sight that met his eyes was both wonderful and confounding. Justin wore a blindfold and was seated on a chair in the midst of several young ladies. He wore a wide grin. A handful of other people stood about the room, some watching the spectacle with amusement, some with disapproval. Wes's main concern was his nephew; what on earth—?

"Good evening, Lord Winterton," said a woman beside him, and he instantly forgot all about Justin.

He bowed. "Good evening to you, Mrs. Cavendish."

She smiled. Tonight she wore a stylish green dress that matched her eyes and displayed her figure beautifully, and he felt a stir of dangerous interest as he looked down at her. "Some of the ladies begged Lord Newton to play a game with them."

"He appears to be enjoying it." Justin said something, too quietly for Wes to hear, but a burst of laughter from the group indicated his nephew was in excellent humor tonight. "Very much," he added wryly.

"The aim of every hostess." She said it lightly, but Wes caught a note of something else in her voice. Tension? Alarm?

Good God, what had Justin done? They'd only been here an hour. "May I present you to the other guests?"

"That would be very kind of you." He offered her his arm, partly out of manners, but mostly out of eagerness to draw her a little closer. She blinked as if startled—and then laid her hand on his sleeve. Even that slight pressure sent a shock wave through him. Wes inhaled deeply, and almost went light-headed on the scent of her: rosemary and lemon. It made him think of Italy, and the hot Tuscan sun above the villa where he'd spent a glorious four months several years ago. He let her lead him across the room.

By the time he made the acquaintance of Lady Serena, the ostensible hostess; Viscount Gosling and Mr. Jones, two visiting gentlemen; Lady Jane Rutledge, a neighbor; and a brother and sister called Penworth who were apparently Cavendish cousins, Wes felt distinctly old. Mrs. Cavendish might be near his age, and Lady Sophronia, an elderly relation, was far older, but everyone else was much more Justin's peer.

That could be taken in two ways. First, advantageously, as it seemed they had stumbled into the exact sort of party that might bring out Justin's more polished side and encourage him to behave in a more appropriate manner.

But second, it also meant far more temptation for his rash and headstrong nephew, and therefore greater risk that Justin would forget himself and do something stupid. Wes felt every one of the eleven years he had on Justin.

"I apologize again for intruding on the party," he told his companion, watching as the young people continued their game.

Her cheeks were the most entrancing shade of pink. "Please don't think of it as an intrusion! I feel certain that if the duke were here, he would have urged you to stay. And I must say, your arrival was very welcome to the young ladies, especially Lady Bridget."

"Yes, she seems very cheerful."

To prove his point, the girl in question let out a shout of laughter, clutching her belly as she did so. "Bravo," called Lady Sophronia, sitting on a sofa nearby.

Wes ducked his head closer to Mrs. Cavendish. "What game are they playing?" he murmured. The bright scent of lemon was driving him to distraction. He wanted to breathe her in forever.

"One of Bridget's inventions, I believe." She wore a slightly apologetic expression. "I'm not certain I can explain all the rules very well—or at all—but the main point is that the blind man"—she nodded at Justin, who still wore the blindfold and a beaming grin—"is presented several clues, and must guess the mystery subject."

"How does one win?"

"By guessing correctly on the fewest clues."

"Ah." He glanced at his nephew. It was clear to see that Justin was enjoying being the center of so much attention. He sat with his hands on his knees, his elbows out, making his shoulders as wide as possible. As Wes watched, Lady Alexandra came up to him and placed her palm against his cheek. Justin flinched, but his smile grew wider than ever.

"Sleigh riding," he said, and the young ladies erupted in applause and giggles.

"Well done," declared Bridget. "Although we should deduct points after Alexandra cheated."

"It's not cheating," protested her sister. "My hands were cold! The clue was cold!"

Justin peeled off the blindfold. "It was the best clue of all," he assured her in his strangely deeper voice. Alexandra smiled, and Bridget rolled her eyes.

"Who shall be next?" She scanned the room. They had clearly been playing a while. "Cousin Viola!"

"No," said the woman next to Wes. "Absolutely not."

"Spoken like a chaperone," he murmured.

"As I am," was her low reply. "Perhaps you should play."

She hadn't said it loudly, but Lady Bridget heard. "Oh yes! Please do, Lord Winterton. We've all had a turn and it's still a quarter hour until dinner."

"Do, Uncle," added Justin with a fiendish gleam in his eye.

Wes glanced at Mrs. Cavendish. Her eyes had widened in surprise, but she recovered quickly. "It won't hurt," she whispered with a rueful little smile. "If you feel adventurous."

God. The blood roared in his ears. That smile did him in, captivating and intimate. Wes heard himself agree before he could think twice. "If it will amuse you." He couldn't resist leaning closer and adding a quiet plea. "But you must give me some hint of what to do."

Bridget hurried over to thrust the blindfold into Mrs. Cavendish's hands. "We'll be sure to choose something clever this time," she said. "Sleigh riding! We can do better . . ." She darted back across the room to huddle with the other young people.

Wes caught the gleeful look Justin sent his way. He turned to Mrs. Cavendish. "Help me," he whispered.

She laughed as they crossed the room to the chair. "It's not difficult." Wes took a seat and she lifted the blindfold, settling it gently over his face. He closed his eyes and took a deep breath as she moved behind him, her fingers stirring his hair as she knotted the cloth. "They will give you clues to the word or saying they've thought of," she said, her voice soft and very near his ear. Wes's imagination began to wander dangerously, conjuring up other ways she could be behind him, her lips near his ear and her hands in his hair. He wondered if the scent of lemons came from her hair or from her skin.

"After each clue you make a guess," Mrs. Cavendish went on. "Lord Newton required nine clues to reach the correct answer, which is the best so far tonight."

"So to win, I need to guess after eight or fewer clues."

"Yes." Now blind, he could still tell she was smiling. "The wittier or more ridiculous the guess, the better."

"Ridiculous?" He turned his head toward her voice. "What do you mean?"

"Lady Bridget thrives on the ridiculous," she murmured.

He would have asked more, but a querulous voice snapped, "Viola! Cease flirting with Lord Winterton and come sit by me. I cannot hear what everyone is saying and you must tell me."

"Of course, Lady Sophronia," replied Mrs. Cavendish. "Good luck," she whispered to him. Wes heard the swish of her skirts as she moved away.

Flirting. He should be ashamed at himself for thinking so, but he wouldn't mind at all if Mrs. Cavendish did flirt with him—blindfolded and otherwise.

"We have decided," announced Bridget then. "Are you ready, sir?"

Wes thought of Justin's little smirk, and Mrs. Cavendish's rueful smile, and of how fiercely he'd played cricket at school. He flexed his hands and said firmly, "I am."

The first clue was *maps*. Still thinking of Viola Cavendish's lemon and rosemary scent, he said, "Italy," which elicited snickers and a hearty "Wrong!" from Bridget.

The second clue was *fire*. Wes puzzled over it until he remembered the admonition to be witty, so he replied, "Christopher Wren." Wren had remade the map of London after the great fire. But his inquisitors only giggled and told him he was wrong again.

The next clue was a dreadful screech, emitted right near his ear, rather like a seagull whose tail was being plucked out. Wes almost bolted out of the chair, but Justin's muffled laughter stayed him just in time. He thought for a moment, decided to be ridiculous, and said, "A history professor who's fallen asleep over his pipe, and set his robes afire."

Lady Bridget hooted with laughter, and the others joined in a moment later. "Better, but still wrong," Justin told him. Wes would have blinked, if his eyes weren't bound shut. Had that been approval in his nephew's voice?

Fourth clue: a gust of air in his face. He thought hard, and said, "A phoenix." There was a moment of silence, which made him hopeful, but then someone said, "Incorrect."

The fifth clue was *Odysseus*, which pricked his interest. Now he began to concentrate in earnest. "Cyclops," he guessed, only to be told he was once more wrong.

The sixth clue took a moment. Wes's mind worked the whole while. Maps, fire, Odysseus, wind, and shrieks. He suspected Justin had put forth this mystery item, to stymie him, and now he was absolutely determined to win. It didn't hurt that he'd caught Mrs. Cavendish's voice saying something quietly, no doubt to Lady Sophronia. It was idiotic and foolish, but he wanted to tear off the blindfold—after he won —and see her smiling at him, surprised and impressed. She was the duchess's secretary, only a few steps up from a servant, but she had the most marvelous green eyes, like the sea after a storm . . .

He was so lost in contemplation of her eyes, it was a total shock to receive a splash of water right on his cheek. Quite a lot of water, actually; it ran down his face and wet his cravat, and there was a dismayed gasp as he reached up to wipe his face. "Bridget," moaned a female voice.

So much for impressing anyone. But the water made him think of the sea after a storm—hang it, also of maps of the ocean, especially medieval ones with illustrations on every corner, and when he said, "Sea serpent," a startled hush fell over the room.

"Am I wrong again?" he asked after a moment.

"Er—no," said Justin, sounding a little nonplussed. "You're correct."

"Near enough, anyway," said Lady Bridget. "It was 'sea monster.'"

"I ought to receive an extra point, for being more precise." Wes pulled off the blindfold, and found he was staring directly at Mrs. Cavendish. She was leaning toward Lady Sophronia but gazing at him, her eyes wide and her lips parted. Their gazes collided and lingered for a moment, then she turned away, a faint pink in her cheeks.

"Well done, Lord Winterton." Lady Bridget stepped forward and offered him a towel. "You trounced Lord Newton and won the round. And I do apologize for throwing a bit too much water."

"I told you no boy would outsmart a man in his prime," crowed Lady Sophronia from her perch beside Mrs. Cavendish. "Didn't I, Viola?"

Her murmured reply was too low for him to hear, alas, as it came just as the butler entered to announce dinner. Lady Bridget bounded forward. "Hurrah! I'm famished!"

"Winterton, you may lend me your arm," announced Lady Sophronia, rising from the sofa. Wes obeyed the command immediately, taking the chance to exchange a quick glance with Mrs. Cavendish. Her eyes glowed with mirth and when she stepped aside to make way for Lady Sophronia, her skirts brushed his leg, sending a charge up his spine.

Good Lord, what was happening to him? Wes tried to focus his attention on the elderly lady clinging to his arm. She was giving directions to all the other guests, pairing them up in no discernible way. She told Justin, a viscount, to give Lady Alexandra his arm, while Lady Serena was assigned to Mr. Jones, a mere gentleman. But no one seemed willing to argue with her, and they went in to dinner.

As he pulled out Lady Sophronia's chair, Wes scanned the table, confirming his suspicion. Sophronia hadn't told Mrs. Cavendish what to do; he'd hoped it was because there weren't enough gentlemen present—counting himself, there were only five, while there were seven ladies—but it appeared Mrs. Cavendish would not be joining them for dinner.

Which was unaccountably disappointing.

CHAPTER 3

The next morning Wes was determined to see if the Duke of Wessex owned the atlas he coveted.

Logically, the most likely place was the library. Even better, at this time of morning he should be able to explore it in solitary peace. Wes had a vague notion that ladies never emerged from their bedchambers before noon, and judging by the silent stillness of the wing where he and Justin had been settled, neither would his nephew. Excellent.

After a quick breakfast in the dining room—barren of all other guests, but laid out with enough dishes to feed a regiment—he asked the butler to direct him. The Kingstag library was on the ground floor, set at the rear of the house. It was a long, narrow graceful room, with tall windows looking out on the snow, still falling thickly beyond the glass. Fires were burning in the hearths at each end of the library, and there were comfortable-looking chairs and sofas arranged at artful intervals. At the far end of the room stood a pair of large globes behind a settee, which immediately caught his eye. He made a note to examine them at a more opportune moment.

Because, unfortunately, he had not discovered the room quiet and deserted. There were a large number of people already there. On the settee before those globes sat Lady Alexandra, smiling and laughing with one of the young ladies Wes dimly recalled meeting last night, and—to his surprise—Justin, who hadn't willingly risen before ten any morning since they'd left Hampshire. Today his nephew seemed quite pleased to be awake, smartly attired and freshly shaved and vying for the ladies' attention with another young dandy. Nearer the doorway where Wes stood, Lady Bridget was pacing, waving her arms as she spoke to Mrs. Cavendish, seated on a chair in front of the windows and studying some pages in her hands.

No one looked up at his entrance.

Wes paused in indecision. Retreat in silence and return later, when he could examine any atlases in the room at leisure? Or stay to see what had put that charming little frown on Mrs. Cavendish's face?

"It makes no sense, Bridget," Mrs. Cavendish said. "You've written lines for a *swan*."

"Does art need to follow every dictate of logic? *No*, I say," declared Lady Bridget. "It is supposed to transport one's soul."

"Obviously," murmured the other woman. "But you must have some sense of story—"

"It's a farce, Viola. They don't need to make sense."

The expression on Mrs. Cavendish's face—perplexed, thwarted, and amused all at once—made Wes want to laugh. He did laugh, in fact, a bare catching of breath in his throat, but it made the lady look at him, her green eyes wide with surprise. He tried to cover it with a cough, then thumped himself on the chest. "I beg your pardon," he said.

"Good morning, my lord." Mrs. Cavendish got to her feet and handed Lady Bridget the pages with a speaking look. The young lady took them to the desk and began writing, scribbling out one long line. Perhaps the swan had lost his part. "Were you looking for someone?"

You. The unexpected thought caught him off guard, and Wes coughed again, a little too hard. "No," he rasped. "I was looking for the library."

She smiled. "You've discovered it! As have most of the other guests. Lady Bridget is working on her play."

"Farce," said the girl, sotto voce.

Mrs. Cavendish closed her eyes for a second. "Were you seeking something in particular?"

"Er . . . A book," he said, unable to think of anything more intelligent to say.

She gave him a patient look. Anyone looking for the library would naturally be seeking a book. "Of course. Have you anything in particular—?"

"No, no, I'll just have a look around. Don't mind me," he said hastily. He strode to the nearest shelf and frowned thoughtfully at it.

"I don't say that the play must be a model of logic and wit, but even a farce has some sense to it." Mrs. Cavendish returned to her conversation with Lady Bridget, her voice lower but still audible to Wes's alert ears.

"This scene has sense! See, the pirate arrives to find the swan sick with love for the lonely spinster, which stokes his own affections for her."

"But on the next page you've got a ghost arriving to deliver a prophecy."

"That also makes sense. He's a ghost because he drowned in a flood. As there's a pirate and a swan, a flood would affect both of them."

Wes choked on another laugh, trying again to make it into a cough. He could just picture the struggle Mrs. Cavendish was undergoing. The ladies behind him fell silent. He realized he was staring at a selection of books about sheep farming, about which he knew nothing and cared even less, and walked to the next bookcase.

Their conversation resumed, even more quietly. "But Bridget, the prophecy is about who shall marry the prince. Where is the prince?"

A gusty sigh, presumably from Lady Bridget. "Viola, there must be a prince."

"Why?"

"I don't know, I haven't written that part yet!"

This time he coughed so hard to cover his amusement, he felt light-headed. It would serve him right if he fainted right here in front of everyone because he'd been eavesdropping. Justin was glaring at him in incredulous outrage, and by the time Wes fished out his handkerchief to mop his stinging eyes, Mrs. Cavendish was beside him.

"I will ring for the maids to dust," she said. "I do apologize, my lord, I'd no idea it was so unpleasant in here."

"Not at all," he croaked through dry lips. Hoist by his own damn petard.

"Then let me send for a cup of tea," she suggested. "I could have it sent to your room, if you wish."

"Yes, Uncle, I do think that would be a good idea," Justin put in from across the room. "You must mind your health, after our long journey here."

Wes glared at him as he stuffed the handkerchief back into his pocket. *Mind his health*, indeed, as if he were a feeble old man. He might look deranged after this, but he was not feeble. "Entirely unnecessary, Mrs. Cavendish. Some fresh air is all I need. Perhaps I'll take a turn in the garden."

"It's snowing out, you know," put in Lady Bridget. "Absolutely pelting down. The doors are probably frozen shut. Tea in the morning room would be far more comfortable."

"Serena and Mr. Jones are in there," said Lady Alexandra.

Bridget's head came up. "Arguing?"

Her sister looked surprised. "No, silly, why would they be arguing? Serena despises him. I think they're rehearsing lines for your ridiculous play."

"Farce," said Bridget.

"A talking swan is ridiculous." The young man beside her raised his brows, and she gave him a teasing smile. "Yes, Lord Gosling, I know you play the swan. I'm sure you shall do your best, but you must admit it *is* ridiculous."

"Not in the slightest," declared Lord Gosling, executing a gallant bow toward Lady Bridget. "All the best actors have played swans. I hope to give the premier portrayal." Lady Alexandra and the girl beside her burst into laughter.

Bridget's mouth thinned. "I shall write something even better for you, Alexa."

The other girl rolled her eyes at Justin, who laughed indulgently. Wes could see very well what was happening there: Lady Alexandra was lovely, and competition always sparked a man's spirit. He tried to send Justin a look of warning, but his nephew deliberately avoided his gaze.

"Are we all to get special parts, Lady Bridget? I could fancy being a prince," Justin said. Casually he propped one foot on the base of the globe beside Lady Alexandra's settee, and rested his elbow on his knee. Wes scowled at the rakish pose.

"It depends." Her gaze moved to Wes. "Lord Winterton, what sort of character would you like to play?"

"I?" he asked, startled.

"Yes, I'm considering adding an elderly king, in the vein of King Lear. I expect he'll have to die so his son the prince can become king. Would that suit you? How would you like to die?"

Justin snorted with laughter. Lady Alexandra smiled, and the other young lady giggled.

"*Bridget,*" gasped Mrs. Cavendish. "My lord, perhaps you'd like to see the house?"

He ought to stay to keep an eye on his nephew. He burned to search the shelves for the Desnos atlas. He did not want to walk away from all the slights on his age and health without protest or at least a show of vigor. Instead he looked into Mrs.

Cavendish's desperate green eyes and said, "Thank you, I very much would."

"I hope you feel better, Uncle," said Justin, as Wes followed her toward the door.

"Have some tea," added Lady Alexandra. "Cook makes splendid tea cakes."

"And stay indoors!" Lady Bridget said just as Mrs. Cavendish pulled the door shut behind them with a bit of a bang.

Viola heaved a heartfelt sigh and rested her forehead against the door for a moment. It was silent and cool in the corridor, although perhaps it only seemed that way to her. What had got into Alexandra and Bridget?

Never mind—she knew very well. Lord Gosling was nothing short of beautiful, and had the most perfect manners she'd ever seen. Viola suspected the dowager duchess had invited the young viscount in case Serena and Frye never made up their estrangement, but Alexandra seemed to have taken matters into her own hands. Add in the also-handsome Viscount Newton, and things could only get dangerous. Viola devoutly hoped the other young people would join them soon and defuse the subtly competitive air between the two gentlemen.

In the meantime she had to deal with the Earl of Winterton, who had just been insulted and practically ordered out of the library. Bracing herself, she turned to face him.

He had a right to be very put out; instead he was grinning, and as their eyes met, he began to laugh. In sheer relief, Viola gave a gasp of laughter herself.

"I'm sorry," she began, trying to regain her dignity, but the earl waved one hand.

"For being a sensible adult in a room full of silly young people? I assure you, your offer of a tour could not have come at a more opportune moment." He made a face. "I could almost feel myself aging and sinking into senility. In a few more moments I would have been relegated to dozing in the corner with a cap on my head, tended by a nurse."

She laughed. She couldn't think of anyone less likely to be found dozing in the corner in need of a nurse than Lord Winterton. Today he was even more handsome than before, if that were possible, his blue eyes dancing with mirth. "The young ladies are a trifle high-spirited at times."

Winterton assumed a tragic expression. "I suppose I've forgotten what it's like to be young and full of life."

"It looks very tiring," she replied in the same grave tone.

His grin returned, and the rogue even winked at her. "For those around them, perhaps."

Viola laughed again in spite of herself. She was astonished at her young cousins' behavior, and was enormously relieved that the earl wasn't taking them much to heart. She ought to have guessed that Lord Winterton, who appeared to be an intelligent and educated man, would seek out the library once confined to the house by the steadily falling snow. Tomorrow she would banish everyone from the room. Perhaps Bridget, if left to write her play without the sly goading of her sister, would embrace some form of sense, or at least hurry up and finish the silly thing.

"If you wanted a particular book, I shall have a footman brave the room to fetch it," she said. "The Kingstag library is exceptional, and I'm sure it can supply something to suit you."

Winterton stared at her with those blue, blue eyes for a long moment. "I rather fancy a tour of the house, as you suggested. If you wouldn't mind."

"Oh," said Viola in surprise. She'd offered in desperation, to escape before Bridget said or did anything to give actual offense. "Of course not." She gestured with one arm. "Shall we?"

He fell in step beside her, hands clasped behind his back. Viola tried to ignore the awareness that rippled through her. She had given many tours of the castle in her two years here; the duke and duchess entertained a steady stream of guests. This should be no different . . . but it was.

"The oldest parts of the castle date from the fifteenth century," she began. "The first duke was given the land for his service to the crown. He was by then a rather elderly gentleman, but his grandson, the second duke, built the central part of the castle."

"The Cavendish family has been in Dorset a long time."

"Yes." Viola opened the door they had reached. "This wing of the castle is relatively new, added only fifty years ago and hence quite modern. Here is the billiard room. Some of the young gentlemen have taken to playing in the evening."

"A fine room," the earl said approvingly, studying the carved mahogany table. It was a very masculine room, done up in the highest quality. Viola remembered her first reaction on realizing the castle held a room dedicated solely to one game—a game no one in the family played much—and quietly closed the door.

"I couldn't help but notice your name is also Cavendish," Winterton remarked as they walked onward.

Her shoulders stiffened involuntarily. She was used to this question, but he must know the answer. She was hardly the first poor relation to be taken in by a family, but it still stung, that reminder—even unintentional—that she had once been mistress of her own home instead of a servant in someone else's. "Yes. My late husband, actually, was a cousin of His Grace." She lowered her voice and gave a rueful smile. "A very *distant* cousin, not one tenth as grand."

"Ah—no. I didn't mean . . ." He grimaced, but with a sheepish grin that made her want to smile back. "I was contemplating how difficult it is to speak to my nephew, and wondering if perhaps you had any suggestions to offer me, since you seem to be in a similar position. Having to advise and reason with your younger relations, I mean."

"Oh!" She made a small motion with one hand, embarrassed but also pleased. "I wish I could say yes, but it's not really the same at all. We're only distant relations, the young ladies and I, and they rightly look to their mother the dowager duchess, or even to the duchess herself, for advice."

"But they don't openly wish for you to leave the room," he pointed out. "At least not in your hearing."

Viola laughed. "Perhaps that's because I have no real authority over them. It renders me utterly powerless to spoil any schemes or plots they may have."

The earl tipped his head in thought. "Perhaps there's something in that. On the other hand, Newton has only held his viscountcy for a few months. He's in desperate want of counsel, whether he admits it or not."

"I have long noticed that often, the more desperately someone needs guidance, the better it is to wait for him to ask for it. Urging your excellent thoughts and ideas upon him only gets the bit between his teeth, so to speak, and sets him against everything you say."

"I see." He gave her an appraising glance. "And do you sit by and watch as they make a muddle of things?"

Viola smiled. As if she had any choice, when it came to Serena, Alexandra, and Bridget. "I find it helps me hold my tongue if I think of the things I did and said when I was that age. It usually quashes my righteous disapproval."

"Good lord," he murmured with a rueful expression. His lips quirked as he gazed at her. "Quite right it would."

Viola could have stood there all day smiling back at him. The realization made her blink and turn away; *do not be too familiar with an earl,* she told herself. She opened the wide double doors to the gallery. "The formal gallery. It contains a portrait of every duke and duchess as well as many other family portraits and mementos. Would you care to see?"

He inclined his head, so she led the way into the long, narrow room and opened some of the shutters for light. No doubt he had a similar room at his own family seat, but he gave every appearance of interest. In the best of circumstances it was a dramatic room, reflective of the wealth and power that had concentrated in the person of the Duke of Wessex over four hundred years. Today it was gray and dim, the snow casting its pall through the tall windows. Viola returned to the door as Winterton strolled the gallery. She didn't want to spend any more time in the chilly room—no fires had been laid in here—but a wicked part of her also took advantage of the opportunity to watch the earl openly.

It was unfair for one man to be so handsome. Lord Gosling was beautiful in a boyish way; the Earl of Winterton was a mesmerizing man in the prime of life. His dark hair was a rumple of unruly waves today, curling over his brow like a classical statue. He paused in front of a portrait, raising his chin to study it, and Viola's eyes skimmed over the lines of his profile. His nose was straight but not large, his jaw firm. He turned to continue his circuit of the room and her gaze drifted lower over broad shoulders, clad in a royal blue coat. His hands, still clasped behind his hips, were elegant, long-fingered and strong. Viola tore her eyes away but not before noticing that his backside was also rather perfectly shaped. She fixed her gaze on the vase on the mantel and kept it there as his footsteps echoed softly in the silent room. *Do not ogle an earl,* she scolded herself. What had come over her?

"A veritable museum of Cavendish history." Lord Winterton returned to her side.

Viola smiled. "Yes. The dowager duchess take a particular interest in maintaining it."

"The lady above the fireplace, I take it." He turned toward the portrait in question, and Viola's attention snagged once more on the sensual set of his lips before she yanked her gaze away.

"Yes. Miss Alice Penworth, when that was painted soon before her marriage." In the painting the dowager duchess was young and beautiful, glowing with love and happiness. It was no secret her marriage to the late duke had been one of love, which had ended tragically some seventeen years ago with the duke's sudden death, when Bridget was a baby.

"Her youngest daughter has her looks."

Viola nodded. "All the young ladies do, to some extent. They have their father's coloring. His Grace looks very like his father, though."

"Does he?" He scanned the walls. "Which is he?"

She glanced at him in surprise. The portrait of the late duke looked almost exactly like the current duke; Wessex was the image of his father, from his deep-set eyes and stern face to his height and build. "There." She indicated the portrait between the windows, at an angle from the dowager's. The arrangement and their respective poses made it appear that the late duke and his wife were gazing in adoration at each other across the room.

"Of course." Winterton went to stand in front of it. "It's very like Wessex, you say?"

Slowly she followed him. "To the life." She hesitated. "Are you not acquainted with His Grace, then?" She had assumed he must be a rather close friend, for the duke to invite him to Kingstag at Christmastime. Wessex was devoted to his family and guarded his time with them closely. The dowager duchess was the one who had planned the house party, and only then because of Serena's recent heartbreak.

"Not really, no," said the earl. He seemed absorbed in the painting. "He's a stern man, I take it."

Oh dear heaven. Had she let a perfect stranger into the castle? The earl claimed to have an appointment, but he'd offered no proof and Viola had never heard warning of his visit from Mr. Martin, who normally kept her apprised of things like that. The duke and duchess preferred their schedules be kept aligned. Her spine stiffened and she said, "I suppose you'll have to form your own opinion."

"Our correspondence was cordial," he said. "And the rumors I heard paint him a passionate, romantic fellow."

The rumors were probably about how the duke had married. Before he met his duchess, Wessex had been engaged to another woman—Miss Helen Gray, now Mrs. Blair. That wedding had been called off at the very last minute, and within days the duke married Cleo and Miss Gray married Mr. Blair. Viola had heard many versions of the story from the Cavendish girls, but she wasn't sure how much truth lay in them. Bridget declared her brother fell in love with his betrothed bride's sister at first sight and pined away until Helen took pity on him and released him from the engagement. Serena believed the sisters had worked it out between the two of them, which one would become the duchess, with all its duties and responsibility, and which one would get James Blair, who was a great favorite of the girls. Alexandra claimed Mr. Blair challenged the duke to a duel over Miss Gray, whom he had been secretly in love with for ages, and the duke stepped aside because *he* was secretly in love with Cleo.

It all sounded highly melodramatic and very unlike the reserved, practical duke she knew. Privately she suspected it had been an arranged marriage between Wessex and Helen Gray in the first place, and once they had a chance to know each other a bit they had realized how wretched their union would have been, a disaster averted in the nick of time. Viola had had many opportunities to see Wessex and Mrs. Blair together, and there was no chance, in her opinion, that either of them could have believed they would suit each other.

On the other hand, one could all but hear the passion crackling between Wessex and his duchess, while the Blairs were the picture of bliss. Whatever had happened, it had certainly ended happily for all of them.

Not that she would ever tell the Earl of Winterton any of that.

"You must judge for yourself," she said again. *Please let the duke and duchess return early,* she silently wished. "Would you like to see the rest of the house now?"

The earl couldn't miss the coolness in her tone. He turned to her, his azure eyes brighter than ever, and smiled—warmly, as if to reassure her. "Very much, Mrs. Cavendish."

CHAPTER 4

*W*es went down to dinner more curious about Mrs. Cavendish than about the location of the Desnos atlas.

His tour of the house had been cut short when a servant came to inform Mrs. Cavendish that the dowager duchess wanted to see her. From the alarm that flashed over her face for a moment, Wes guessed that his absent hostess was keeping an eye on things from afar. But the end result was that his companion excused herself, and he didn't set eyes on her for the rest of the day.

It left him free to amuse himself, and he did try to redirect his thoughts toward the Desnos. After a calculated delay, he returned to the library. This time only Lady Bridget was in the room, pacing and muttering to herself. At his entrance, she stopped short.

"I beg your pardon," Wes said with a slight bow. "Mrs. Cavendish was called away, and I hoped to find a book to read."

The young lady pressed her lips together, but curtseyed. "Of course. I was about to go to the drawing room anyway. Do come in, sir, and help yourself to any books you fancy." She went to the desk, gathered her papers, and left.

Wes stood back as she went by him. He hadn't meant to chase her away, but he wasn't about to protest being left alone in the library for a while. He headed straight for the globes, presuming any travel books would be there.

An hour of hunting did not turn up the Desnos, nor any atlas which might be mistaken for it. He stood drumming his fingers on the table, wishing he could ask Mrs. Cavendish. She must know. She appeared to know everything that went on in the house.

And yet he doubted she would tell him, even if she knew precisely where the Desnos was. He had been mesmerized by her, and felt an unwarranted eagerness to take a tour of Kingstag Castle when she offered. But he hadn't missed the chill that came over her demeanor after he revealed that he didn't know the Duke of Wessex personally. She wasn't merely the duke's employee, she was also a relation. The widow of a distant, lowly cousin, in her telling, but one who clearly took her familial connection seriously.

Wes had distant relations who turned to him for support or assistance. He supposed he employed some of them; he'd been away from Winterbury Hall so much, he wasn't entirely sure. He *was* certain none of them were members of his personal household, and he was quite sure none of them were remotely as attractive as she was.

Mrs Cavendish, though, was a member of the family here. He eavesdropped on her easy conversation with Lady Bridget with amusement, but also envy. His discussions with Justin were never so affectionate or so . . . so . . . peaceful. It was genuine curiosity in part that drove him to ask her advice.

Wes didn't think too much on the other reasons he felt like seeking her out.

When he reached the parlor where the guests were gathered before dinner, Justin gave him a severe look. Wes ignored it. Mrs. Cavendish was engaged in conversation, so he skirted the throng of young people, biding his time, and as he did so another lady caught his eye.

"Good evening, ma'am." He bowed before Lady Sophronia.

She looked him up and down. "Winterton! It's about time. You may sit with me; all the handsome men do."

Amused, he took the seat next to her on the sofa. Lady Sophronia was tiny and must be over ninety, but her hair was still elaborately arranged, and dyed an unnatural shade of red. Unlike many elderly ladies who clung to the fashions of their youth, she wore a modern gown, although with the most unusual cape over her shoulders.

She noticed him looking at it. "Otter," she confided, stroking it gently. "A gift from my second fiancé. Such a fine man he was; Russian, you see, and so virile."

Wes blinked. "Indeed."

"Have you been to Russia?" She nodded at Lady Alexandra, who was holding court for Justin and some of the other young people by the windows. "Alexandra tells me you're quite a world traveler."

"I have been to Russia, ma'am, though only once, and not for long. I prefer climates warmer than England, not colder."

She gave a snort of laughter. "Missed your mark this time! There hasn't been this much snow at Kingstag in decades. I should know, I've been here for seven of them."

"Have you really?" he said in admiration. "You must know everything there is to know about the castle, then."

Her gaze turned sharp. "More than likely. What's sparked your curiosity?"

Unconsciously he glanced at Mrs. Cavendish. She was speaking to the eldest Cavendish girl, Lady Serena. "Nothing specific," he said absently. "Mrs. Cavendish very kindly took me on a tour of the house today."

"Did she? Viola's a good girl." Lady Sophronia nodded. "Wretched luck, of course, but she's got spirit. I like her."

"Wretched luck?" Wes tried to look only mildly interested, even though he'd gone tense and somehow concerned. Did Sophronia only mean that she was a widow? Reduced to working for wages? What bad luck had Viola Cavendish suffered?

The elderly lady shook her head and wagged her finger at him. "It's not my place to tell you her life story. If you want to know, you'll have to get it from her."

Wes sat up a little straighter. "Indeed, Lady Sophronia, I meant no offense—"

She cackled with laughter. "No, of course not! You can't keep your eyes off her. I may be old but I'm not blind. She's a pretty girl . . ." She paused, her head tilted thoughtfully to one side, and gave a small shrug. "Not a girl, I suppose, but certainly young enough to be foolish about some things. Well, I'll tell you this: her husband—a good lad, James, but no head for money, and a man without money is hardly worth marrying—was Wessex's third cousin. Their great-great-grandfather was my uncle, and a duller person you never met. He was a Calvinist and as a consequence never spent a farthing on anything frivolous in his life. What a waste!" She shook her head, looking piqued. "He left his children provided for, but James . . . The men in that branch of the family are handsome as anything, but idiots, all of them, each in his own way. Thank goodness Wessex inherited some sense with his title, or we'd all be living on turnips and roasted squirrels. Have you ever eaten a squirrel?"

"Er." Wes blinked at the diversion. "No. A crocodile once, on the banks of the Nile. But James . . .?" For once he had no interest in talking about his travels.

Sophronia seemed pleased. "Crocodile! How exotic." She gave him a triumphant smile. "I knew you were not a dull person. I have no patience for dullards. You must tell me more about Egypt, and your visit to Russia. I always longed to see Sergei's homeland. A Cossack shot him before we could marry. Such a cowardly thing to do. A proper duel with swords would have been at least romantic and exciting."

"Of course," he said, trying once more to get the conversation on more interesting topics. "I take it Wessex was close to his third cousin?"

"What? Oh no, he barely knew the boy." She frowned. "Such a pity. James's grandmother was my bosom friend. We had such times together! But she had a weak heart, as did all her family; they died young, every one of them I can remember. Naturally Wessex would look after James's widow, but Viola was the one who insisted on a position."

"She seems part of the family." He watched as the woman in question spoke quietly to Lady Serena, who smiled warmly in return and clasped her hand for a moment. "Quite warmly received."

Sophronia scoffed. "She knows how to make herself useful! I do admire that in a person, you know; people who know how to do things are wonderful to have around."

"Then it seems a very fortunate thing for all, that she's here."

"Indeed," said Sophronia. "As for how long she'll stay . . ." She raised her shoulders. "Well, necessity will guide that, I suppose."

Wes tried to look only politely curious. "Necessity?"

Sophronia glanced around furtively, and lowered her voice. "Oh yes, she has very good cause to stay for now. Later? Who can say. But she'll likely not see reason, not where *he's* concerned."

"Ladies and gentlemen, shall we go in to dinner?" Lady Serena blushed and smiled prettily as she made her announcement. At her side, Mrs. Cavendish gave a tiny nod of approval, and even the butler looked proud.

Wes mustered a smile and helped Lady Sophronia to her

feet. She waved him away and summoned Lady Bridget, who hurried over, and they began a quiet but animated conversation.

He strolled off, wondering what she'd meant. Who was *he*? Why was Mrs Cavendish only in her post because of *him*, and why was she unreasonable about him? All in all, Lady Sophronia had only inspired more questions than she'd answered.

Well. Perhaps he was unreasonable for being so interested. If he wanted to know more about the lady, he ought to own his interest honestly and speak to the woman. He was nothing but a gossipy bore if he pried into her history from afar and never made an effort to know her. And if he became less interested as a result of that effort, then he neither deserved or needed to know every detail of her past.

He would just have to keep reminding himself of that every time she smiled at him.

CHAPTER 5

For the first few days of the party, Viola felt confidently in control. Serena was doing an admirable job as hostess, Bridget's ideas for entertainments stayed within the bounds of propriety, and even Sophronia was behaving herself. Every day she reported to the dowager duchess that all was well.

By the third day, the novelty of the deep snow began to wear off. Alexandra snapped at Serena, who told her to go sulk in her room if she couldn't be civil. Lord Newton and Mr. Jones got into a testy argument about sleigh racing. One of Serena's dearest friends, Miss Kate Lacy, arrived at last after being delayed by the storm, but so did a mysterious young man called Conte Luigi Mascapone. Viola knew he was not on the guest list and despaired of what to do with him, but Lady Sophronia clasped him in her arms, declared he was the grandson of a dear friend of hers, and invited him on the spot to stay for the party. Viola could do nothing but send the housekeeper to prepare a room for him.

Lord Winterton seemed to be either hiding from the young people, which Viola could somewhat understand, or fascinated by Kingstag; more than once she bumped into him in some unusual part of the house. He claimed to be lost, which was reasonable, but she was beginning to wonder how such a world traveler had such a poor sense of direction.

The last straw was catching Bridget doing something suspicious in the library on the fourth day.

Viola didn't actually know what Bridget was doing. She went to inquire how the play was progressing—by then she was in desperate search of anything to occupy the rest of the guests, and Bridget had holed up in the library promising to have a new act ready before dinner for people to rehearse. But when she opened the door, Bridget was not at the desk, writing diligently on her play. She was standing in front of an open French window, letting powdery snow blow into the room.

"Bridget!"

With a startled motion the girl slammed the door. The glass shuddered so hard Viola feared it would break.

"What are you doing?" Viola hurried across the room. Snow was blowing against the glass, and the wind blew loudly against the castle walls, throwing up white powder that sparkled in the weak winter sun.

"Getting some fresh air." Bridget widened her eyes innocently and went back to the desk. She dropped into the chair and bent over her papers, scribbling away.

Suspicious, Viola scanned the terrace outside. She could see no one, but were there footsteps in the snow leading from the door around the corner? It was hard to tell in the glittering breeze. "Was someone here on the terrace?"

"In all this snow?" Bridget scoffed. "Who would traipse through it?"

"That isn't an outright denial."

Bridget made a face, her pen still skimming across the page. "I suppose if you think someone might decide to wander through the snow to chat through an open window, there's nothing I can do to dissuade you. Go out and search, if you like."

Viola was certain the girl was lying, but there was nothing she could do. She turned the lock on the French window just in case, and went back to the desk. "How is the play coming along? Everyone is quite anxious to have more scenes to rehearse."

"It's bloody brilliant," said Bridget with satisfaction. "Original and ridiculous and everything a farce should be. Read this." She pushed some pages across the table.

Viola picked them up and began reading, only to catch a slight motion from the corner of her eye. Bridget had slid something beneath the blotter. Her eyes narrowed, but she kept her mouth closed. She'd got into a battle of wills with Bridget before and always ended up completely routed. There was no one here, and as Bridget had said, the snow was much too deep for anyone to have snuck into the Kingstag gardens and up to this terrace.

That said, Viola would have wagered a week's salary that Bridget had been talking to someone through that open door.

"It does sound ridiculous," she commented after reading the scene Bridget had given her.

The girl beamed. "Doesn't it? And so fitting for Serena."

Viola read again. "That she's pursued by a swan?"

"Well, that's what Frye is," Bridget replied. "Handsome but cruel."

"But Lord Gosling plays the swan, not Frye."

"Drrr!" Bridget rolled her eyes. "Obviously I could not write a part for Frye, because he's not here. Gosling will do just as nicely, though. I don't care for him."

"Because . . ." Viola couldn't even think of a reason.

"He's too agreeable! Whatever odd thing I write for him, he smiles and carries on. Agreeable men are so very disagreeable, don't you think?"

She laid the pages back on the table. "If you say so . . ."

Bridget beamed again. She knew she'd won.

On the fifth day things slipped a bit further out of control. Lady Sophronia had taken over supervising the play rehearsals, with Bridget's help when the latter wasn't off in the library writing, and Viola was shocked to see her almost encouraging Mr. Jones, playing a pirate from Shropshire of all places, to kiss Serena, playing a maiden—or, as Bridget insisted on calling her, a Lonely Spinster. The kiss wasn't called for in the script, although the pirate did bear away the maiden at some point, but Viola was alarmed by this. She managed to insert herself into the direction and even the acting twice, but finally Sophronia pinned a gimlet gaze on her.

"Dear Viola," she said, "I have not seen Lord Winterton in an age. The poor man, he must be feeling very put out to arrive and have no one to look after him."

Viola blinked. "Lady Sophronia, he's quite comfortable. He assures me so every morning." Viola looked forward to those brief meetings over breakfast; it was easily the most pleasant conversation she had all day. Her worries about the earl had subsided. He might not know Wessex personally, but he was clearly a gentleman and had behaved with the utmost propriety.

But he *had* been strolling all over the castle, and Sophronia's words planted a seed of doubt. Perhaps she had neglected him. She could hardly blame the man for avoiding the antics of the young people, who were scouring the castle for props and costumes and—Viola was sure—a bit of mischief whenever possible.

"Balderdash," said Sophronia bluntly. "A man won't say when he's bored, Viola, he shows you. Winterton has been wandering the corridors like a lost child. I'm very much afraid he shan't give a good report of our hospitality to Wessex."

Viola's lips thinned at this transparent effort to get her out of the drawing room. "I am sure Lord Winterton understands the circumstances."

"But do you want to chance it?" Sophronia looked past her as Viola reeled. "Bridget! What have you got for us today?"

"A new scene, but we lack any suitable props." Bridget plopped onto the sofa beside her great-aunt. Sophronia leaned her head close to see the pages she held. Viola had long since decided that Bridget was Sophronia reborn, exuberant and irrepressible. "Viola, could you help locate them? Everyone else is busy rehearsing."

She shifted uneasily. The pair of them were looking at her so innocently, it immediately put up her guard. "What do you need?" Perhaps it could be found swiftly and she could be back before anything untoward happened . . .

Bridget consulted her pages. "A large book, a cape—preferably red velvet; what do you think, Aunt Sophronia?"

"Oh yes, definitely red velvet," said the old lady in delight.

"A set of goblets that may be thrown around and not break, and an iron chain."

Viola, having listened in growing dread, blinked at the last. "An iron chain?" she cried. "Bridget, what's in this play?"

"A ghost," said Bridget patiently. "I've told you that for days. But we haven't got a chain, or a crown—"

"A crown?"

"He's the ghost of the king."

Viola put one hand to her temple. "You said the ghost delivered a prophecy *about* the king."

"Yes. And then the king dies and becomes another ghost." Bridget smiled as if she'd just answered every question. "And the prince becomes king after that, you see."

Viola stared helplessly. "Of course."

"There must be a chain and a crown somewhere in the

house," Bridget went on. "It is a castle, after all. Ask Mama if you cannot find them on your own." She paused, then added, in a markedly offhand manner, "Perhaps Lord Winterton would help you look."

Viola glanced at Sophronia, who merely gave a tiny smile and nod, and knew she was stuck. "Very well, I shall ask him. But you must promise to behave," she added in a lower voice.

Sophronia waved both hands. "Of course! Of course!"

"No more kisses on stage," Viola added, casting a glance at Serena and Mr. Jones. Serena was talking to Lord Gosling, but Mr. Jones was watching her with a strangely pensive expression. She was afraid the kissing would give the poor man ideas, which would be unfortunate. Frye might be despised as a scoundrel by Alexandra and Bridget, but Viola knew the dowager duchess still hoped Serena's erstwhile suitor would return and persuade her to mend the broken engagement.

Bridget rolled her eyes. "We need the chain desperately. Otherwise Mr. Penworth will have no way to rehearse his scene, which is vital to the plot."

"We cannot have that," said Sophronia at once. "Viola, I am certain no one can find these things as quickly as you can."

Viola very much doubted there was a plot to this play, but she couldn't overrule Lady Sophronia. She nodded and went to find the earl.

He was in the small parlor near the grand hall, admiring a book of engravings laid out on a table near the windows. He glanced up as she came in, and a broad smile crossed his face. "Mrs. Cavendish. How does our grand entertainment progress?"

"I cannot speak to its grandiosity, nor to it being entertaining," she said wryly. "I have been sent in search of props, and hoped I might enlist you as well."

"Of course." He closed the book and faced her. "What are we in search of, and where should we begin?"

"That's why I need help," she replied. "A most ridiculous list, and I haven't the first idea."

His eyes lit up and he grinned. "Excellent! An adventure."

"That it will be," she agreed, and they set out.

One item was easily accomplished. A visit to the kitchens and a few words with the cook unearthed some tinware that the actors could throw and not break. Viola told a footman to take it to the drawing room where the play was being staged, and they went in search of the next item.

"A scarlet cloak," mused the earl. "Surely one of the ladies has a suitable one?"

Viola hoped so. By good luck they ran into Miss Penworth on her way to the music room. She was very talented on the pianoforte, and Bridget had assigned her the task of choosing and playing dramatic music for the play. Viola had lost all reserve by now, and spurred by Lord Winterton's suggestion, she asked Miss Penworth if she or any of the young ladies had brought a red cloak. Fortune smiled on her; the young woman had brought such a cloak, and promised to send it to the drawing room.

"Thank you," said Viola fervently. "I hope Lady Bridget's play does no harm to it."

Miss Penworth laughed. "I've known Bridget all my life," she confided. "If it does, I am already well aware that His Grace will replace the cloak. He replaced my doll when Bridget drowned it in the lake, two bonnets lost to escapades planned by Bridget, and more hair ribbons than either of us could count."

Viola breathed a sigh of relief as they left Miss Penworth to her practicing. "Two down, three to go."

"What's next?" the earl wanted to know.

"A crown, a large book, and an iron chain." She shook her head. "A chain! Perhaps in the stables?"

They paused before a window overlooking the park in front of the house. The snow had stopped and the sun had come out, but the scene was no less daunting. It looked like a foot of snow drifted over the grounds, with only a few tamped paths through the glittering whiteness. Getting to the stables, down near the lake, would be cold and slippery.

"Perhaps in the attics?" The earl cocked his head toward her, his eyes dancing and a wry smile on his lips. "Or the dungeons?"

"There is an armory, but no dungeons I know of." She tapped one finger on her lips, thinking.

"Dare I ask why a chain is required?" The earl appeared in no hurry to keep searching. He clasped his hands behind him and stood watching her. "It seems an odd item in a farce."

And that is why Bridget wants it, Viola thought. "There was mention of a ghost—two ghosts," she amended. "One will be the dead king—hence the crown—and one will be . . . another ghost." His lips curved. Against her will, Viola's did the same. "I've absolutely no idea why she wants a chain," she confessed.

"Is that the weak, infirm, dead king I'm to portray?" he asked, as if dreading the answer.

She tried to stop it, she really did; but a gasp of laughter escaped her, then another. "I'm terribly afraid so," she said, her voice shaking.

Winterton sighed and hung his head as Viola bit her lips to keep the laughter bottled inside her. "At least I'm to be a weak, infirm, and ultimately dead *monarch.* Having been here a few days, I now know it could have been so much worse. A dead night-soil man, or a pickpocket."

"Well. Yes." Viola tried to speak normally. "But the king leaves a crown for the prince, while a pickpocket . . ."

"That depends on his skill at picking pockets, don't you think?" The earl grinned impishly. "He might leave a ruby the size of a hen's egg."

She laughed again. "Or a tatty old handkerchief."

"Ah, but it's the chance of something more exciting that renders it interesting. I think Lady Bridget would agree with me."

Viola shook her head, but still smiled. "No doubt. Bridget would write a scene having him pick the pocket of a mikado or a rajah, as simple as you please, in the heart of Westminster."

"A rajah! Now that would be an interesting role." The earl's face lit up. "I've been talking to young Mr. Jones about India, as he intends to take a diplomatic post there."

"Does he?" Viola hadn't heard that about Mr. Jones, only that he was friends with the scoundrel Frye and therefore must be hateful, according to Alexandra. She also claimed he'd said something very unkind about Serena, but from Viola's observations, he hadn't meant it.

"Yes. He asked for my advice on the journey there. I gather Newton has told everyone I've traveled to every corner of the globe, and can't bear to set foot in England." He said the last with a grimace.

"Have you?" Viola blushed when he looked at her in surprise. "That is, I did hear that you are a great traveler. I've never been out of England, and can't imagine what it's like in India."

"Do you long to see the world?" he asked, sounding interested.

She thought for a moment. "A little," she replied at last. "Yes, I suppose I do. I never had the chance of it." A clock chimed in the room behind them, making her guiltily aware that she was doing nothing, just standing in the corridor talking to the earl. "Shall we see if there is a suitable large book in the library?"

"Of course."

"It's not true that I can't bear to set foot in England," he said abruptly as they walked. "I've been home for almost a year now."

"So long," she murmured.

"So few people truly get to see the world," he went on, almost as if trying to persuade her. "There are places so vastly different from England, one can hardly describe them. People so different than Englishmen. Art and food and music. I would hate to spend my entire life without seeing anything other than the village I was born in, perhaps a few other villages, and then only London for exotic sights."

That rather perfectly described Viola's own life. "How very fortunate that you were able to see more." She opened the doors of the library. Bridget had completed most of her play, so everyone was off rehearsing in other rooms. The library was quiet and empty.

"I do feel fortunate." The earl went to the French windows, opened the drapes, and gazed out at the snow. The wind had died, and the view was dazzling. "Those who have the means and the ability and the desire to travel ought to do so, to bring those far corners of the world home to those who stay."

"So it's your duty?" She smiled to take the sting off the words, but he still shot her a sharp glance. Viola put up her hands. "I don't judge, my lord. You have the means and the desire; therefore it's entirely your choice whether you stay or not."

"Wouldn't you go, if you could?"

Her smile turned wistful. "Perhaps. Perhaps not. Everyone dear to me is here in England. It hasn't felt like a great loss to remain home."

He recoiled as if struck. "I didn't mean it's a loss to stay home."

"And I didn't mean it's an indulgence to travel." She hesitated. "Lord Newton is young. Life seems to pass so slowly when you're young. You feel you will go mad if you can't escape the ordinary drudgery of home and family. It's only when you're a bit older that you realize how easy it is to lose those things, sometimes without noticing until it's too late.

"I expect he's told everyone you're impatient to be gone because *he* would like to explore the world—at least a bit of it beyond England's shores—and because of his father's death he cannot. He sees you as free to do as you please, and if he were free to do as he pleased, he would be on the first packet to France." She stopped at his expression. "That is only my guess at his feelings."

"No," he said slowly, still staring at her. "No, I believe you're correct."

Viola felt her face heat. "You know him much better than I—"

"I doubt it." Winterton's eyes were piercing. "I've only seen him a dozen times since he was a boy."

"Well." It was astonishing how flustered she felt, just from him looking at her. "Perhaps you'll become better acquainted with his thoughts and feelings during this visit." She chewed her lip and changed the subject. "A large book. Perhaps an atlas would do?"

He tensed. "Pardon?"

"An atlas. Bridget said it must be a large book, and an atlas is the largest book I can think of." She went to the bookcase and surveyed the selection behind the finely carved wooden screen. "Perhaps this one. It's large and looks impressive." She pulled it from the shelf and opened it on the wide table.

The earl stepped up beside her. "Absolutely not."

"Why not?"

"It's Cellarius's *Harmonia Macrocosmica*, and shouldn't be trusted to Lady Bridget's farce. I'm astonished Wessex keeps it here among the other books."

Viola gaped as he took the book and turned gently through a few pages. His face was bright and sharp with interest. "This is one of the most beautiful examples of celestial cartography in the world. Look—" He laid one page in front of her. "The northern sky."

It was a beautifully illustrated page, in vivid colors with constellation figures sketched over a background of stars. "It is lovely," Viola whispered in awe. "I'd no idea it was particularly valuable."

"I suppose not everyone would think so." He closed the book reverently and put it back on the shelf. "Is Wessex a collector?"

"I'm not privy to that. The duchess has a fondness for maps, but I've never heard her speak of the stars."

Winterton went still, as if startled. "Maps?"

Viola smiled. "Yes." Before her marriage, the duchess had owned a prosperous draper's shop in Melchester, and she'd stocked a good number of exotic fabrics from around the world. Viola had seen the map that used to hang in the shop offices, with pins pressed into the countries where she got her fabrics: fine cottons from America and India, silk from China, jacquard from France. Now that she was mistress of Kingstag, someone else ran the shop, but she still took an interest in it.

"I also have a fondness for maps." Winterton turned around, his head cocked curiously. "I've never met a duchess who shared it. Does she collect them?"

"Do you?" Viola asked brightly. On no account would she discuss the duchess's personal interests with him. "I suppose you must, on your travels."

"I do have a number of them," he admitted with a grin. "Atlases and maps are marvels—an entire worldview contained in one page or one book. I have an atlas of the world that doesn't include any hint of America, because it wasn't known. Another ancient map is centered about Jerusalem, per the church's preference. And others—such as this Cellarius—are maps of things we can never possibly visit."

"Yes," she murmured, struck by his enthusiasm. "But you would like to."

"To visit the stars? No." His gaze grew distant. "But they are a traveler's dearest companion. The same stars that shine above home in England also shine above the Indies, the Americas, and China. Every sailor learns to chart his way using them as a guide. In that respect, a map of the stars is more valuable than any map of the land."

Viola couldn't stop a small wistful sigh. She was perfectly happy here in England—mostly—usually—but the excitement in the earl's face as he spoke of sailing the seas and seeing exotic lands and people did plant a tiny seed of envy in her heart. Just to have the chance to go on such a journey would be incredible.

But she did not have that chance, and probably never would.

"You find the prospect appealing," said the earl, his gaze returning to her with keen discernment.

"A little," she allowed. "Well—yes, I do. Perhaps not to travel all the way to China, but to see Paris, or Venice, or some of the mountains in Switzerland . . . *yes*, it does sound thrilling." She turned back to the shelves to break the moment. *Do not be tempted by a wealthy earl's questions*, she told herself. "What would you suggest we give Bridget, if none of these are suitable to being props?"

The earl turned to the bookcase. "Are these all the atlases at Kingstag?"

"Yes." Too late Viola remembered that the duke had bought another recently as a gift for the duchess. It was a finely bound atlas, with all the trading routes around the globe marked, and the duke thought his wife would be charmed by the drawings and engravings of items from far-off lands. It mirrored the map she had kept of where her goods came from.

But that was to be the duchess's Christmas gift, and as

such could not possibly be flaunted in Bridget's play. Viola had been sworn to secrecy by Wessex, who was quite pleased with himself for thinking of something so unusual for his wife.

The earl seemed disappointed by her answer. A thin line appeared between his brows as he stared at her for a moment, almost as if he knew her answer wasn't entirely correct, but he said nothing. After a moment he pulled a book from the shelf. "This one."

"An almanac of last year." Viola grinned. "No one will be tempted to read it during the play, I suppose."

Winterton's mouth twisted ruefully. "Not in the least."

W es didn't know what to do. For a moment he'd thought he would finally get a look at the Desnos atlas, to see if it was the one he sought.

There were only a few known editions of the Desnos atlas, all dated from the previous century. They were handsomely illustrated and annotated, which would have made one desirable enough to a wandering soul like his. But the particular atlas he sought had belonged to his father.

Wes had spent hours poring over those maps, listening to his father's tales of the sights he'd seen in those remote and exotic locations. When the late earl died, the atlas has been mistakenly sold with some other books and Wes had been searching for it ever since, making inquiries of collectors and dealers all over England. After years of no success, he'd heard the Duke of Wessex might have it. The duke's reply to his queries had been vague and not very encouraging, but Wes was undeterred. He'd learned the duke was a family man, which meant there was a chance he could be persuaded to sell it by Wes's story—and that was enough chance for him to travel to Dorset, in winter, with his surly nephew in tow. He was determined to have that atlas again.

But it was not in the Kingstag library, and now Viola Cavendish had just said there were no other atlases in the castle. Her face, though, had gone blank for just a moment after she said that, as if remembering something. Perhaps she suspected there was another?

He thought hard about it as they went about the remaining tasks. They delivered the almanac to the players in the drawing room and found the housekeeper, who promised to send a footman to the stables in search of a chain. He trailed after Mrs. Cavendish as she scoured a storage room, finally holding up a battered piece of metal with a pleased exclamation.

"Will this serve as a crown, do you think?" she asked, lifting it above her head.

"Hmm? Yes." He had to know about that atlas, but was it better to ask her now, or wait until Wessex returned and ask the duke directly?

Some of the humor left her face at his curt reply, and Wes immediately regretted it. "A fine crown indeed," he said more heartily, reaching for it. "Does it suit me, since I'm to be the doddering old king who wears it?" He set the thing on his head and crossed his eyes.

She smiled uncertainly. "Very well, sir."

"Then a crown it is." He took off the cylinder, which had probably once been part of a chandelier, or perhaps a base for a glass dish. It was tarnished and bent now.

"We should get Lady Bridget's approval before congratulating ourselves." She headed toward the door.

"Mrs. Cavendish?" She paused, but didn't look back. "I apologize," Wes said. "For my abruptness."

"Oh no, my lord," she began, but he made a low noise in his throat and she fell silent.

"May I confide in you, ma'am?"

Slowly she turned to face him fully. "Yes, but . . ."

"But your loyalty lies with Wessex; I know." He smiled

wryly. "You must have wondered what brought me to Kingstag in the middle of winter." She said nothing, but her green eyes were fixed on him. Wes thought he might drown in those eyes, and knew he was doing the right thing by being honest with her. "I am looking for a particular atlas Wessex may own. He may not, but neither of us knows for certain. I came to Kingstag to see if it's the one I desire, and if so, if I can persuade Wessex to sell it."

"What sort of atlas?"

Wes's face softened in memory. "A very dear one, to me. It's a Desnos atlas, which are not common, but neither are they very rare. But this one was once my father's. He died while I was away—Tahiti—and by the time I returned home, it had somehow been consigned with other old books and sold. My mother didn't know it was anything special, but that was the atlas he showed me when I was a small boy. It inspired my interest in foreign lands, from the wild Americas to exotic China. I would like to have it back, for the notes he wrote in the margins, his observations of other peoples, tales from his voyages—" He stopped, unexpectedly overwhelmed.

"Was he a great traveler as well?" she asked softly.

Wes nodded. "Not as much as he would have liked. He took me on my first voyages around Europe. My mother and sisters stayed home, but he took me, a raw stripling without two ounces of sense." He grinned, shaking his head at the memories. "As I grew older I went with others and some-times off on my own, while he returned home to manage Winterbury Hall. Much as I did when he died."

Mrs. Cavendish crossed the room. "I'm very sorry you lost him, sir."

"Call me Winterton," he said, savoring the blush that colored her cheeks. "And thank you."

"I understand why you wish to reclaim the atlas," she went on. "I probably shouldn't say so, but the duke recently bought an atlas, as a gift for the duchess. He isn't likely to sell it, whether or not it was your father's. Are you certain the one you seek isn't among the others in the library?"

"I had a look the other day," Wes admitted, "and didn't discover it. The bookseller I contacted in London said he'd sold a Desnos atlas only recently to Wessex."

Mrs Cavendish looked at him with compassion. "I don't think he'll sell it," she said again.

Wes mustered a smile. "I shall have faith as long as possible."

"Perhaps it's not even the same one."

"Perhaps." But he suspected it was. "I don't suppose you could show me the one Wessex bought recently?"

She drew back. "No. I don't even know where it is. His Grace asked me a few questions when he was searching for a gift for Her Grace, but I had nothing to do with it otherwise. I know nothing except that he thought the maps and illustrations in it would appeal to Her Grace."

"The Desnos atlas does have splendid illustrations."

She chewed her lip for a moment. "I'm sorry I cannot help you."

Wes opened his hands wide. "I didn't expect you to do more than you have. I shall have to wait until Wessex's return to see if it is my father's old atlas, and if I can persuade the duke to part with it."

"I wish you luck," she said softly. "His Grace is devoted to his family. He might understand."

Wes couldn't help smiling back. "Thank you, Mrs. Cavendish."

There was an odd moment as they stood there beaming at each other. Even though she'd all but driven a stake through his hopes, confirming that Wessex likely did have the atlas while at the same time making clear why the duke was very unlikely to sell it to him, Wes found himself feeling happier than he had since arriving in Dorset. There was something about her face that made him want to smile every time he caught a glimpse of her. She was lovely, but it was more than that; her face was full of kindness and humor and so expressive, he could gladly sit and watch her without saying anything at all. But when she smiled *at him* . . .

Good lord, he was in trouble.

"We should present the crown to Bridget," she said.

"Right." Wes put the makeshift crown on his head, tilted it to a rakish angle, and folded his arms. "As the late, desperately unlamented ruler of this realm, I command it."

Her face lit up and she laughed. Her nose wrinkled a bit when she did, and his heart gave an odd thump. "You're taking your demise very well, my lord."

"Given that I have no choice, I shall accept my fate gracefully, as befits a monarch." He took the crown from his head. "Perhaps it will serve as a good example for the prince." As hoped, Justin had been given the part of the prince, although Wes still had no idea what that role entailed. Not that he knew what his own role entailed.

"Lord Newton has made himself very agreeable." Mrs. Cavendish closed the storage room door behind them as they headed back to the drawing room.

"He is improving," Wes admitted. Justin had been in excellent spirits since they arrived. Perhaps Anne was wrong to keep him at home so much. Wes certainly hadn't wanted to be at home when he was twenty. He'd gone to Egypt with two of his mates from university that year.

"He's charming," said Mrs. Cavendish diplomatically. "I daresay the young ladies are very pleased you brought him to Kingstag."

Wes laughed. "At least I did something to redeem myself!"

"Oh no! You are most welcome, Lord Winterton!" She put her hand on his arm. Wes stopped in his tracks, as did she. He stared into her sea-green eyes, and again his heart took a strange leap.

Good lord, he was in trouble . . . and it was exhilarating.

With a muffled gasp she snatched her hand away, and without thinking Wes caught it. "Thank you," he whispered, raising it to his lips for a kiss. "For I find myself very pleased that I came."

CHAPTER 6

$\mathcal{A}$fter the electric moment with the earl, when he caught her hand and looked at her as if he'd like to pull her back into the privacy of the storage cupboard and kiss her senseless, Viola tried to busy herself with dull tasks in the distant reaches of the castle. Not because she feared the earl actually would pull her aside and kiss her senseless, but because she was coming to hope he might.

Her hand had tingled for an hour where his lips brushed it. After she delivered the makeshift crown to Bridget, she fled the drawing room, even though it left Sophronia completely in charge. The earl had watched her go—Viola could swear his gaze made her feel warm and giddy from all the way across the room—but thankfully he didn't follow. That was proper, she told herself; she was a servant and he was a gentleman of leisure.

So she ended up sitting in the small room off the duchess's private parlor where she normally worked, staring out at the snow and wondering about the foreign lands Lord Winterton had been to. Had he seen the ancient pyramids in Egypt, which Stephen said were marvels of engineering? Had he been to India and seen elephants? Lord Newton had told the young ladies fantastical tales of his uncle's journeys, and as much as Viola reminded herself it was not her place to know, she burned to ask him about all the places she had read of, but would never see herself.

It was true that everything and everyone she held dear was in England. Even more, the dearest person in the world to her, her brother Stephen, relied upon her being prosperously employed, and that was easiest to accomplish in England. She had neither means nor opportunity to go abroad, whether she wished to or not. Unlike the earl.

She sighed, brushing her fingertips over the knuckles he had kissed. Everything about her life was unlike the earl's. She was an idiot to sit here thinking a kiss on the hand meant anything. He was being polite, or flirting, or even trying to persuade her to help him locate that atlas. Not that she didn't understand his desire to have it. She'd made sure Stephen got their father's astrolabe and sextant, and she'd kept her mother's pearl necklace, which would have paid for a term at Cambridge.

But whether or not the duke would be willing to sell the atlas, if he even had it, Viola knew she ought to stay out of the matter. Her growing sympathy for and interest in Lord Winterton could only get her in trouble.

She was still torn when she went down to dinner. It was part of her duties to help oversee dinner and entertain the guests in the drawing room before and after the meal, but she was not expected to dine with the guests. When it was just family, she was often invited to join them, but during this party she receded to her proper place.

Naturally the first person she set eyes on when she reached the drawing room was Lord Winterton. No one else was in the room yet, so she felt safe enough returning his smile.

"How did the rehearsal progress?" she asked.

His eyes closed for a moment, as if in pain. "Apparently I die a very bloody death, though thankfully off stage."

Viola giggled before she could stop herself. "I trust you're quite regal and imposing before that."

"Pompous and boring, I should say. 'Let not my subjects make merry,'" he intoned. "'There is too much frivolity in the kingdom, and I will have an end to it.'"

"Oh my." Viola wondered what on earth Bridget was thinking. "To what end?"

"Solely to *my* end," he replied dryly. "My role is to be pompous and boring, die savagely, then return as a ghost after the prince becomes a far more beloved king, to penitently pronounce that I was wrong to be so pompous and boring, but now I shall rest in peace because the new—much better—king has brought such joy and merriment to my former kingdom."

Viola burst out laughing.

"I do not recall actually agreeing to be in the play," the earl went on, although he was smiling now as well. "I suspect my nephew wrote my entire part, and I can only be grateful the rest of the guests shall be actors in the play as well, and not sitting in the audience watching."

"I am so sorry," Viola gasped, wiping at her eyes. "Lady Bridget is quite fanciful . . ."

"And Lady Sophronia is even worse!" he exclaimed quietly. "I shouldn't say this, but I believe she patted me on my—er—hindquarters."

Oh merciful God. Viola herself had noticed, more than once, that Winterton had exceptionally fine—er—hindquarters. And she knew Lady Sophronia had an eye for such things. "Perhaps it was inadvertent," she suggested weakly.

Winterton gave her a look. He didn't think so.

God save her. Viola could feel her face turning red. "I'm so sorry," she said again, her voice shaking as she tried desperately not to laugh again. She could picture exactly how Sophronia would have lined it up.

Winterton's face eased. "I took no offense. She reminds me greatly of my grandmother, who used to say she appreciated a pair of muscular calves on a man. She paid her footmen a bonus if they were strong runners, and not because they could deliver her messages faster. I hope I live to such a great age, when I may say what I like and not care a whit what others think about it."

"I suspect Sophronia reached that age seventy years ago," murmured Viola. "Thank you for being such an excellent sport about the play."

He grinned. "When one travels, one learns to accept the unexpected and make the best of it. Often those surprising turns lead to the most memorable experiences of the journey. I find Lady Sophronia charming."

Viola let out her breath in relief. No wonder Sophronia had patted his bottom; she must have recognized Winterton would let her get away with it. "I do as well," she whispered, "but not everyone does."

Winterton laughed. His eyes were so blue and friendly, and Viola found herself smiling back at him. Again.

The other guests came in then, discussing the play rehearsal in good spirits. Bridget had somehow procured a bucket of white feathers, and stuck them all over a coat and cap for Lord Gosling to wear in his role as a Lovesick Swan. The effect was quite ludicrous, but Gosling took the teasing in stride with a smile, declaring that he thought it a very handsome costume since Lady Bridget had made it herself. Bridget rolled her eyes at his flattery, but Viola could tell she was pleased. Bridget was pleased whenever anyone embraced her mad ideas.

When the butler announced dinner, Lord Winterton made sure to offer Lady Sophronia his arm. Viola's heart gave a funny little jump at the easy way he had with the older woman. Sophronia *was* charming and amusing, when approached the right way—any sign of shock or indignation, and Sophronia would dig in with relish, purposely being even more shocking and inappropriate.

Viola went to take her own dinner before it was time to return to the party, to instill some order and decorum to whatever after-dinner activities Bridget persuaded Serena to do.

Tonight it was charades, which was perfectly acceptable. Viola settled at the side of the room and watched in amusement. As usual, Bridget's riddle was ridiculous and took a very long time to guess. When Serena finally called out "chalk figures for dancing" and Bridget nodded, a small cheer went up.

"I wondered if anyone would ever solve it," said a voice beside her.

Viola glanced at Lord Winterton. "Someone always does," she assured him. "Lady Serena knows her sister well."

They both turned to watch Serena, taking her place at the front of the room and pondering her riddle. She looked happier, Viola realized. The grave quiet air she'd worn for weeks after her engagement ended had vanished, and when she smiled at something Miss Penworth said in jest, it was open and warm. It brought a small curve to Viola's own lips; all three Cavendish girls had become like younger sisters to her, and she took their sorrows and joys very much to heart.

"I heard she was recently disappointed in love." Winterton sat on the settee beside her, his voice low enough no one else could hear. "She seems to be recovering."

"Happily, she does."

The earl glanced at her. "I heard the cruel young man was even invited to this party."

Bridget, Viola reflected, had no discretion at all. "He's not cruel," she murmured in reply. "He's young." Young, handsome, and a very dashing duke. She didn't know why the Duke of Frye had ended his engagement, but she couldn't believe he'd done it to be cruel to Serena. Their families had been close for ages. And Serena didn't look very broken-hearted anymore . . .

"Is there no chance of reconciliation?"

Winterton's question startled her. "Oh! I'm sure I don't know. But Frye hasn't arrived, as you can see, so at the moment I rate it very low odds. He can never be forgiven if he never comes to beg forgiveness."

He grinned. "Nor should he be." For a moment they watched as Serena delivered her riddle. "Do you have an interest in the stars, Mrs. Cavendish?"

Viola blinked. "Stars in the sky?"

"Yes."

"A little." It made her think of Stephen. She had to blink back a sudden tear at the thought of her brother.

"Come with me," the earl said. "It's terribly cold, but the sky is beautiful. I thought you might like to see it."

Her lips parted in surprise. And delight. After all, her brother might be looking at the same stars tonight. It was two days before Christmas, and it was the closest thing to sharing it with him she might have. "All right," she said.

She cast one glance over the room as they slipped out. Everyone was absorbed in charades. Sophronia was watching from her usual chair near the hearth, and there was a great deal of mirth and laughter. A little devil on her shoulder whispered that no one would miss her for a few minutes.

Viola followed the earl to the doors at the back of the hall. In the summer they often stood open, presenting a beautiful vista over the gardens, bowling green, and the ancient oaks that lined the road to the stables. Tonight all those sights were covered in piles of snow, and the raw air made her eyes water as they stepped out. She clasped her arms around herself and stayed close to the door, sheltered from the wind.

"It's a bit cold," said the earl sympathetically, looking unaffected by the temperature himself. "But look." He raised his arm and swept one hand across the skies.

She put back her head and gasped. It had been snowing heavily all evening, but now it almost looked like a hole had opened in the sky. Clouds still ringed the horizon and hovered over the tops of the trees, but directly above them was a jeweled canopy of stars, sparkling against the black velvet of the night.

"There is Polaris," said the earl, pointing. "And there is Sirius." He pointed toward the far left horizon.

"Goodness," breathed Viola. "You can see everything! There—look—the Cork Nebula lies there!" In excitement she pointed as well.

Winterton looked at her in amazement. "The Cork Nebula! How do you know that?"

"My brother is studying mathematics and astronomy at Cambridge," she said, still gazing raptly at the stars. "The Cork Nebula is at the heart of Perseus. There is Pegasus, and Lyra, and—oh—such a beautiful view of Vega!"

The earl's eyes moved back to the sky. "I have no idea which stars are in Pegasus," he said after a moment. "I only know a few points of navigation."

"That's not even one star in a thousand," said Viola with a laugh.

"What else do you see?" He stepped closer, until their shoulders were touching. Viola felt the warmth of him beside her like a roaring fire.

Stars. She focused on the sky and pointed east. "There is Pollux." It was easy to find, nice and bright. "And there south of it is the belt of Orion. The Spanish call them Las Tres Marias. The ones in asterisms are easier to find."

"Marvelous," murmured the earl, his head tipped back, giving her a perfect view of his profile.

"Stephen would have spent every night outside, pointing

them out to me. Our mother made him come inside, and he would sleep under an open window, even in the dead of winter." She smiled in memory.

"Mathematics and astronomy. How impressive."

She nodded. "Stephen's brilliant. I wouldn't be at all astonished if his name is as famous as Mr. Herschel's some day."

The earl was staring at her. "I'd no idea you had a brother, Mrs. Cavendish."

"Only one, younger." She raised her brows in fun. "Ought you to know all my family?"

He laughed ruefully. "Forgive me. Of course not. I have inflicted my family on you, and that really should be enough."

"Inflicted! Lord Newton is hardly that bad . . ." She paused at his expression. "Perhaps writing a painful death for you as king was a bit much."

He snorted. "What is your brother like?"

"Brilliantly clever," she said at once. "We knew from the time he was six that he should go to Cambridge. My father was a sea captain, and he taught Stephen how to navigate by the stars."

"A sea captain! And you never had the desire to go away?" The earl clasped his hands behind him and studied her with interest.

She smiled wistfully. "I never had the chance! Females, I was told, are not very welcome on ships . . . But Stephen went on a few journeys with him, where he noticed nothing but the stars overhead. Once my father showed him how to use the sextant—well! My brother barely pays attention to anything on earth now when an idea seizes him. His passions are stars and nebulae and planets, how they move and how they change appearance, and how he might possibly improve his telescope so that he can see them better. When he's working on a calculation, he forgets to speak to anyone, to eat, even to sleep."

Winterton shook his head in amazement. "I always admired those fellows at university."

"I can't even imagine an entire college of them," she said honestly. "Stephen alone amazes me."

Winterton chuckled. "I doubt one chap in ten at Cambridge works that hard at his studies as all that. But here —you're shivering."

Viola realized she was. "We'd better go back inside."

He opened the door and touched her back lightly as she went back in. Viola felt that touch through all the layers of cloth between them. *Do not make anything of it,* she told herself. "Thank you," she told the earl as he bolted the door behind them. "For showing me the sky."

"It may be snowing again by morning."

"I know." Viola smiled. "But it was beautiful for that moment."

His blue gaze felt like a caress on her face. "Yes. Very beautiful." She flushed with pleasure, as if he'd paid her a great compliment. He reached up and gently brushed a few flakes of melting snow from her hair. "Like the night Of cloudless climes and starry skies; And all that's best of dark and bright . . ."

Kiss me, she thought, feeling herself falling into his mesmerizing eyes. Viola stopped breathing as the force of the thought hit her. "Marlowe?" she asked breathlessly, trying to jolt herself out of it.

"Byron, I believe." He fingered a loose curl of her hair, studying it for a moment before smoothing it behind her ear. "We could check, in the library."

The library would be dark and deserted and private now. Anything might happen there, just between the two of them. She should go back to the charades, remember her duty, and not let poetry and starlight go to her head. Slowly she nodded. "Yes. Yes, we could."

Something shifted in his focus. He knew what she meant. He offered his arm.

Do not be stupid, Viola told herself. But she put her hand on his arm and went with him.

CHAPTER 7

Wes's pulse seemed to be pounding against every inch of his skin. Her hand was on his arm, and her eyes were glowing like emeralds, and he'd never seen anyone more beautiful than Viola Cavendish, standing in the frigid night, head thrown back to gaze at the stars. Her lips had parted in wonder, and Wes had nearly kissed her right then and there.

It was all he could think about now. That, and her hand on his arm as she went with him on the most specious errand ever invented. He knew very well it was Byron's poetry he quoted, but for a half hour alone with her, he'd happily check every book of poetry from Marlowe, Jonson, and Shakespeare. If they weren't distracted before locating the poetry books, that is . . .

They reached the tall double doors of the library. She picked up a lamp from a nearby table as Wes reached for the doorknob.

But a lamp already burned inside, on the desk by the near hearth. The two people in the room looked up, startled, and in a flurry of movement flew apart.

Not, though, before Wes saw who they were and what

they were doing. Lady Alexandra was frantically smoothing her dress back into place. Justin ran one hand through his disheveled hair, but seemed to realize it was hopeless. His jacket was off, his cravat was askew, and he gave Wes a glance that was half sheepish, half defiant.

Wes shut the door with a bang.

"Uncle, let me explain," began Justin.

"Close your mouth," said Wes in a deadly soft tone. "I will speak to you later. Lady Alexandra, are you hurt?"

Her flush was visible even in the low light. "Not at all, sir."

"What is going on?" Mrs. Cavendish finally found her voice.

Lady Alexandra looked frozen. Justin cleared his throat. "It was not nearly as bad as it looked."

"No?" Mrs. Cavendish turned a frigid gaze on him. "What was it, then?"

Justin opened his mouth, seemed to realize the problem, and closed his mouth.

"It was only a kiss," said Lady Alexandra in a quavering voice. "Just a little one."

Mrs. Cavendish looked pointedly at Justin's white shirt-sleeves. They must have been alone here for some time. Wes could have smacked himself for not paying more attention to Justin's interest in the girl. How long ago had they snuck away from the party in the drawing room? Alexandra had been sitting on the desk, Justin's hand on her knee—thankfully on top of her skirts—and her arms around his neck. It probably *had* only been a bit of kissing, but Lady Alexandra was the daughter of a duke, a young lady who was expected to make a very good marriage and have a spotless reputation.

And if that reputation became tarnished and stained by Wes's feckless nephew, there would be hell to pay.

"I hope your mother Her Grace agrees," Mrs. Cavendish told Lady Alexandra.

Alexandra shot her an agonized look, but nodded. Viola reached for her arm and drew her firmly toward the door.

"Mrs. Cavendish . . ." Justin's voice was hesitant. "Truly it was my fault. I asked her to come away from the party . . . Blame me."

"I do, sir," she said bluntly. "But it is not my response you need to be concerned about." She swept Alexandra out the door.

A full minute of silence reigned in the library. Justin didn't seem to know where to look. Wes counted to ten to save his temper from erupting. "What the devil?"

He must have mastered himself better than he thought, because a slight smile crossed Justin's face. "She's very pretty."

Wes stared at him stonily.

"She's great fun too."

Wes maintained his stare.

Justin began to wilt. "It was naught but a little kiss."

"Don't you ever say that to me again!" Anger finally boiled over. Justin flinched as Wes advanced on him in a fury. "Go to your room and stay there. Do not speak to anyone. Do not ring for a servant to remove your boots. Do not do *anything* but sit quietly in your room. If I can't trust you to do that, we leave tomorrow morning even if we must climb through snowbanks higher than our heads, carrying our baggage. Do you understand?"

"Yes, Uncle," Justin muttered.

Wes continued to glare at him. "I will attempt to smooth things over as much as possible. If you leave your room before I come speak to you, I shall find a switch and thrash you like the boy you clearly still are."

"Yes, Uncle," Justin whispered.

Wes grabbed his jacket from a nearby chair and flung it at him. "Go."

Justin's ears were red as he tugged his jacket back on and ducked out of the room.

Wes paced for a few minutes. Bloody hell. Was that boy's head completely empty? What was he thinking?

He had to stop himself there. Of course he knew what was in Justin's head; much the same desire had been beating away at Wes's own brain. If not for Justin, he might be kissing Viola Cavendish right now . . .

But that was a totally different situation, he argued to himself. He was not a green boy and she was not an innocent young lady. They both knew what they were doing. If he kissed her, if she kissed him, it would be because they both wanted it . . .

He sighed. It didn't really matter. And he suspected that how he handled Justin's indiscretion would have a large impact on whether he'd ever get another chance with Viola.

Viola kept a firm grip on Alexandra's arm as she hurried down the corridor toward the dowager's apartment. The only way for Alexandra to head off any trouble over the kiss was to confess it immediately to her mother, before a careless comment or whisper could blow the whole thing out of proportion. Viola also hoped the experience would leave a lasting impression on the girl and prevent her from doing it again.

"Viola, I'm sorry." Now Alexandra was full of contrition. "But it was only a little kiss! Nothing more. Surely you don't think I'd forget myself enough to do worse."

"I don't know anything. You slipped away with a man and went into the dark library, which looks very guilty. Girls have been ruined for doing that."

"Ruined! It was nothing!"

Viola stopped. "A little kiss is nothing. But what would have come next?"

Alexandra blinked. "Nothing! Newton would never—"

"Perhaps not, but you don't know him well enough to be certain of that. I would hate to see you make a terrible mistake next time."

Alexandra flushed from her neckline to her ears. "Next time?"

"If you can do it once, you can do it again. The next time a handsome man whispers pretty words in your ear and begs you to sneak out with him, you'll be more likely to go. After all, you got away with it before and bore no consequences." Viola raised her brows at Alexandra's shocked expression. "Don't tell me it's impossible. In London there will be many handsome men wanting to dance with you and kiss you, and some of them will not have restraint or honor."

"But I never have a chance to do anything!" the girl protested, tears thickening her voice. "I'm always behind Serena, waiting for her to find a husband. Well, now she's been jilted and I'm still waiting. All the gentlemen look at her first—next spring even Bridget will be out with me, and I shall just be the Cavendish sister in the middle. I'll end up like Aunt Sophronia—"

Viola rolled her eyes. "Only if you wish to."

"Newton's very handsome! And eligible! Don't you think Gareth would approve of him, if he knew?" she argued.

"If he knew," repeated Viola with meaning. "I shan't speculate on what your brother might do or say, *if he knew,* since neither you nor Lord Newton took the time or trouble to seek his approval before sneaking off for a bit of kissing. What do you think he'd say now?"

Alexandra bit her lip. "I shall explain to Mama. Mama will understand."

"I hope so." Viola was relieved that Alexandra had grasped the import of this moment. If the dowager could see that it was a harmless kiss, nothing much would come of it. No one else had seen anything, and even if the other guests had noticed Newton and Alexandra leaving together, that was proof of nothing. Viola could even say she had been with them, if it came down to it.

Of course, if the dowager grew upset that her daughter had been able to sneak off with a gentleman, there was one person to blame for failing to chaperone her: Viola.

They had reached the dowager duchess's suite of rooms now. Viola put her hands on the girl's shoulders and gave her a firm squeeze. "Chin up. Your mother was once a young woman, hoping to fall in love, flattered by a handsome young man's attentions. She will surely understand what you're feeling. But that's no excuse to be foolish, and risk your reputation for a few moments of excitement. And don't blame Lord Newton; unless he carried you off to the library against your will, you are as much to blame as he. You are a young woman now, Alexandra, and must take responsibility for your own actions. Be honest and true with your mother, and I have faith she'll treat you fairly."

The girl stared at her with dark, worried eyes. "Isn't it monstrously unfair that such a trifling thing could cause such trouble?"

Yes. Viola felt uncomfortably aware of all the impure thoughts she had had about the Earl of Winterton recently, and how easily she could have been the one caught kissing in the library. He found her attractive; she sensed that if she gave him any sign, he would kiss her. Perhaps do more. Perhaps she had even agreed to go to the library with him because she knew he wanted to kiss her, and she wanted him to do it.

But she had even more to lose than Alexandra did. "Yes, but that won't change anything. 'It's not fair' is rarely a winning defense."

A spark of pique animated her face for a moment. "It should be. Lord Newton won't be judged so harshly over a trifling little kiss."

Viola sighed. "His uncle looked very displeased with him. But that doesn't affect you, which is why you must speak to your mother before anyone else does. Own your mistake and learn from it, so you don't make a worse one later."

Alexandra wilted. "All right." She put back her shoulders and knocked on the door. It opened almost immediately, and Ellen let her in. Viola waited until the maid had closed the door before she let out her breath.

CHAPTER 8

Viola dutifully returned to the drawing room, but thankfully everyone else was ready to go to bed. No one asked where Alexandra or Lord Newton had gone, although Sophronia did murmur something about Lord Winterton with a sideways glance at her. Viola let it go. Tonight had been hard enough already.

So she did something she rarely did and helped herself to a bottle of port from the tray in the drawing room, then climbed the stairs to her rooms and shut the door.

Just looking at her apartment gave her a pang. The duchess had given her a luxurious room by servants' standards, a comfortable bedroom with an adjacent sitting room. It was small, but it was private and it was hers. Even more, it wasn't on the servants' floor but tucked at the end of the corridor where the duke and duchess had their rooms, almost like a member of the family. That was to make it easier for her to answer the bell that hung discreetly near her bed, of course, and it was right next to the servants' stair, but it still made all the difference. She could pretend that she was more Cavendish than servant.

It was shocking how quickly her happily settled life might go to pieces.

With a sigh she dropped onto the chair near the hearth and poured herself a glass of port. What were the odds the dowager would be upset? Viola had always admired the dowager duchess's levelheaded approach to things, but there was no telling what she might do when one of her children was in trouble. The poor woman was still ill, growing frustrated at her inability to recover, and every day she peppered Viola with ever more detailed questions about the party's progress. She was very annoyed that Frye had not arrived yet. The match between Serena and Frye had been arranged by their fathers years ago, and the dowager duchess still clung to hope that Frye would arrive, fall on bended knee to apologize profusely for breaking the engagement, whereupon Serena would graciously forgive him and fix a date for the wedding.

Now Viola faced the possibility that the dowager was about to be greatly disappointed by two daughters instead of one. Serena displayed no interest in Frye's attendance, and Alexandra was sneaking off to kiss a young viscount she'd only met last week. Anyone would be upset in these circumstances, and Viola knew she was the most likely person to bear the blame.

What would she tell Stephen if she got sacked? She took a large sip at the thought. Her poor brother. If she could have held on for another two years, he would have been able to finish his studies and become eligible for a post at the university. That was where Stephen belonged, among the books and scholars and ancient stone buildings that had harbored the likes of Isaac Newton. What would he do, out in the real world? He was brilliant enough to be a professor and witty enough to be a dean . . . except when his brain went off on some wild and wonderful journey through the realm of astronomy and mathematics. She'd known him to stay awake for three days straight, barely eating, working away until his hands were black with ink and he looked like a wraith from the grave. She'd given up scolding him about it years ago; he told her it was like a hurricane in his head, and he would have no peace until it blew itself out. Nor did he want peace from it—on the contrary, he reveled in those storms of thought that swept him away from her and everyone else on earth, into the exotic and thrilling world of numbers and stars and all sorts of things that enchanted him, but bewildered everyone else.

Alas, hurricanes of thought didn't pay well. James, her dear James, had been so fond of Stephen. His affectionate kindness for Stephen, then only a gangly lad, had been what initially endeared him to Viola. When she married him, James had pledged to pay for Stephen's schooling, and off her brother went to Cambridge.

But that came to an abrupt end when James's heart gave out. His income was only for his life, and it turned out he hadn't saved much for his widow—not that he'd had time, dying before his thirty-seventh birthday. Viola had been staring poverty and ruin in the face, and Stephen the loss of his place at Kings College.

The Duke of Wessex offered her a small stipend when she applied to him for help, as James's most illustrious relation, but it wouldn't have been sufficient to support both her and Stephen. Viola had swallowed her pride and asked for a position instead, with a regular, higher salary. As a secretary, she was able to send to Stephen enough for his school fees and books. If she instead had to pay for her own lodging and keep . . .

The tap on her door roused her from her growing anguish. She went still, suddenly gripped by fear that the dowager duchess might be sending for her already.

"Mrs. Cavendish?" called a low voice. "Viola?"

She gasped in relief, and went to open the door. "Good evening, sir. Do you require something?"

The Earl of Winterton stood there, looking penitent. "I wanted a word, if I may."

Viola dipped a shallow curtsey. "If you please, sir, perhaps Mrs. Hughes or Withers—"

"No!" He lowered his voice and ran one hand over his hair, ruffling it into unruly dark curls. "I wanted to talk to *you*."

She gripped the doorknob. The servants at Kingstag Castle were expected to be as respectable as the family. Socializing and romantic attachments were permitted, but only when conducted with propriety and decorum—and inviting the earl into her private rooms would be neither proper nor decorous. And she had just scolded Alexandra for doing much the same thing with Lord Newton.

On the other hand, letting the earl sit on her sofa for a few minutes could hardly make things worse, if the dowager duchess decided to sack her. She opened the door wider. "Then you might as well come in."

Winterton frowned. Viola gave a small shrug and went back to her chair. She propped her foot upon the fender and waved one hand toward the tiny table by the fireplace. "Have a glass of port, m'lord."

Slowly the earl stepped into the room. "You're upset."

Viola tilted her glass at him. "No," she corrected him, "I am resigned."

"To what fate?" He closed the door behind him.

Viola looked hard at that closed door, decided it didn't matter enough to protest, and sipped her port. "The duchess left me in charge of the household. Yes, Lady Serena is acting as hostess," she acknowledged as his brow dipped. "But she's not accustomed to maintaining order in a household this size. Naturally Her Grace the dowager duchess is, but she's still stricken in bed. Hence, the duchess entrusted me with the running of the house in her absence."

"That's a weighty responsibility."

She laughed weakly. "Isn't it? I assured her I could manage, even with the guests and the snow and Lady Sophronia being let off her lead. And I *was* managing well enough, until—"

"Until my nephew and I arrived," he finished when she didn't. "I will speak to the duke. Newton will speak to the duke and he will do whatever the duke deems proper and necessary."

Viola felt herself droop. "Proper? You know as well as I do what that normally means, my lord. But you are not acquainted with the Duke of Wessex."

Winterton hesitated. "No, I've never met him."

"Then allow me to offer you some advice, when you do meet him." She rearranged her feet on the fender. The fire was very warm. "He adores his sisters. He will throw over propriety and every rule of society to protect them, and a viscount who's still wet behind the ears will be no match for him."

"What are you saying?"

"I am warning you to tread carefully, and for heaven's sake tell your nephew the same. The duke will not be pleased to learn he trifled with Lady Alexandra."

"I imagine not." The earl came another step into the room. "May I?" He gestured at the sofa. Viola waved one hand in assent, and he took a seat. Any fluttering awareness she had of the man should be entirely overwhelmed by the disaster that loomed before her.

Still, he sat very near her. When he stretched out his own legs, his boots brushed her skirts. As if from a distance she watched the fabric sway, then settle. Goodness; the port must be having an effect on her after all. She turned her head to look at the earl, and discovered him watching her.

She guessed what he would say. *What ought I to do to keep the duke from calling out my nephew?* Viola had not seen the

Duke of Wessex in a temper often, but he was not a meek or indecisive man.

"What will happen to you?" Winterton asked instead.

It took a moment for the question to sink in, which then caused her to sink lower in the chair. "Me? I might be sacked."

"Why?"

"You know why," she said softly.

"Hear me out," he responded, calm and unruffled. "Lady Alexandra has been flirting with Newton all week. Putting them together in the same house for days on end in a holiday spirit was bound to foster some interest between them. It's only natural."

"And it's only natural that His Grace will be furious." She sipped more port.

"But why would he sack *you*?"

Viola swirled her port, then drained the glass. "I ought to have kept a closer watch on Lady Alexandra."

"And I on Newton." Winterton blew out his breath. "His mother will have my head for this, you know. I thought I'd outgrown my fear of her, but tonight I am discovering that I have not."

She peeked at him. He looked glum but serious. "His mother is your older sister?"

"By several years, and she entrusted her son to me on the condition I would teach him some restraint and dignity." He grimaced. "She'll box my ears and slap my face, just as she did when I scalped her favorite doll."

Viola's eyes went wide. "Scalped!"

For a moment something like guilty enjoyment flickered over his face. "I fancied myself an American native, like the ones I read of in travel diaries. They cut off their enemies' hair, did you know? Anne can be a bit . . . managing, and at the age of six I decided she was my mortal enemy. Obviously I could not cut off her hair, but her doll . . ." He flexed one hand and shrugged. "It seemed a good idea at the time. She was too old for dolls then, yet she took it oddly to heart."

Viola laughed. It was wrong to laugh, both at the story and because she might still be in an ocean of trouble, but once she started, she couldn't stop. She laughed until her sides hurt and she was gasping for breath and her eyes were wet. And when she finally recovered enough to catch her breath, she discovered she'd crossed the line into sobbing at the end.

The earl had gone down on one knee in front of her. He held out a handkerchief without comment. Viola took it and blew her nose, loudly and miserably.

"Is there a chance you're underestimating Wessex's understanding and compassion?"

She rolled the damp handkerchief into a ball. "Perhaps. It will depend, I suppose, on what Lady Alexandra tells her mother. If the dowager duchess takes umbrage, she will urge the duke to do the same."

"What will Lady Alexandra tell her, do you think?"

Viola thought of the set expression on Alexandra's face as she went in to see her mother. "I expect she'll say it was a trifle; some harmless flirting, a stolen kiss."

"As it most likely was," he pointed out.

Viola sighed. "She's a proper young lady, the sister of a duke. She's not at liberty to flirt with and kiss any young man she chooses."

"No." He looked down. "If I may repeat my question . . . What will you do?"

"If I'm sacked?" He gave a slight nod, and she put down her glass. "Look for another position." She looked sadly around the room. "I'm very fond of this one, though. It will be hard to leave Kingstag."

He nodded, rubbing his hands on the arms of her chair. Viola covertly watched. He had lovely hands, strong and big. "Would it reassure you," he said very slowly, "if I promised you a similar position at the same salary?" She jolted, and he raised those lovely hands as if to calm her. "Only if you cannot find one more to your liking. I hate to think you might be brought low by my nephew's actions, and thus by my own. I blatantly invited myself to Kingstag, and then I brought Newton with me. If there is blame to be laid, I must accept my share."

"You don't need to do that, my lord," she murmured.

"But I want to." One corner of his mouth tilted upward. "I want to very much, actually."

Viola turned her gaze to the corner of the fender where her feet were propped. *Do not become enamored of an earl*, she told herself. Especially not this earl, with his strong hands and endearing grin and an offer that could easily lead her to forget herself and do something very wrong, like flirt with him. Encourage him. Let him kiss her, and kiss him back, repeatedly, until she ended up in bed with him, begging him to make love to her. She didn't want that, she really didn't, even though part of her *did* want it, despite it being a terrible idea and—

A knock at the door startled her out of those thoughts and sent her leaping to her feet. She looked in alarm at the earl, who had also risen. There was no way to excuse his presence in her private room.

Without a word, he pointed at her bedroom, brows raised. Viola gave a quick nod, ignoring her conscience, and he stepped quietly inside, closing the door behind him. Straightening her shoulders, Viola went to the main door and opened it.

Alexandra stood there. Her eyes were a little wet, but she managed a smile. "May I come in?"

"Of course." Viola stepped aside and followed her to the tiny sofa.

"Mama said I must apologize to you," the girl began. "I put you in a very bad spot, and betrayed your trust. Mama was terribly upset that I took advantage of your distraction to steal away, when she's been so sick and you've had to do so much more than usual." She sucked in a deep breath. "But I want to apologize for myself. I know it was wrong, and even though nothing very improper happened, I'm sorry I did it. As soon as I saw your expression, I felt so stupid." She pleated her skirt, her whole figure drooping. "I hope you don't think less of me."

"Of course I don't." She clasped Alexandra's hand. "I understand exactly—what's more, I agree that it isn't fair a mere kiss should be judged so harshly. But I don't make the rules, and I would hate it more if you suffered. I may not be your sister—or your brother—able to protect you in other ways, but you are very dear to me, Alexandra."

Alexandra gave her a grateful smile. "As are you to us, Viola. I told Mama several times it was not your fault, and she agreed it was all mine." She made a slight grimace. "Jane always says her mother would sack a companion who allowed her to get into trouble, but I won't let Cleo think ill of you. I don't want you to go, and I shall try very hard not to put you in that position again." She paused. "What you said, outside Mama's door . . . Thank you. I had been feeling rather put out lately—everything has been Serena, Serena, Serena. I *want* her to be happy, I do . . . and I shall never forgive Frye for breaking her heart, *never* . . . but I was beginning to feel impatient with all the fuss over her. This whole party was arranged to cheer her up, and she doesn't even seem sad to have lost Frye." Her mouth quivered. "I shall try to be a better sister."

Viola pulled her into a hug. "You *are* a good sister. What happened to Serena was dreadful, but she shall survive it—as shall you survive this little to-do." Alexandra smiled. Viola squeezed her hand. "I fear we're all going a bit mad, trapped inside by all the snow. Who knew it could snow so much in Dorset? I've never seen the like . . ."

Alexandra laughed at last. "Nor I." She got up. "Mama

said she doesn't want to make a fuss over a kiss—as long as I have learnt my lesson. I shall keep Lord Newton at a distance and be more conscious of my actions."

"Very good. That's all any of us can do." Viola walked her to the door. "Good night, Alexandra."

"Good night." Alexandra left, and Viola closed the door, feeling vastly relieved. If Alexandra escaped this with nothing worse than a scolding and chastened spirits, all would be well.

She had not forgotten that the Earl of Winterton was in her bedroom. He must have heard her conversation with Alexandra, and his mind must be at ease about his nephew. If the dowager duchess saw no reason for upset, there would be no need to tell the duke. That would put her own mind at ease, of course; if she didn't lose her position at Kingstag, there would be no need for her even to think about Winterton's offer, and what it might lead to, and why he'd said he wanted to propose it to her very much.

She opened the door and paused. It was a small room, barely big enough for the bed and a washstand, with a clothes cupboard in one wall. Consequently, Lord Winterton had stretched out atop her bed, his long legs crossed, his arms folded behind his head. There hadn't been a man in her bed since James died two years ago. The sight sent a shock of desire through her, hot and so powerful she had to cling to the doorknob to keep herself steady.

"She's gone," she said, shocked by the low husky quality of her voice.

He sat up and swung his feet to the floor. "I heard. All will be well?"

He was relieved the duke wouldn't thrash his nephew. "It seems so."

Winterton nodded. He still sat on her bed, far too big and masculine for her widow's room. Viola was trying without much success to stifle the wicked thoughts drifting through her mind like snow, a veritable blizzard of sinful images threatening to swamp her composure. She shouldn't have drunk that port; it had shot her good sense to flinders.

"Then you won't be sacked," said the earl.

Viola cleared her throat. She hadn't even been thinking of that. "I feel less anxious on that score."

He smiled again, that roguish grin that made her heart skip beats and her mind go blank. "And vastly relieved you shan't have to address what I said earlier."

She was too distracted by the sight of him sitting on her bed, his large, lovely hands clasped between his knees and his coal black hair rumpled as if he'd just woken . . . in her bed . . . "Yes, of course."

He got to his feet and came toward her. It only took two steps but they seemed very momentous and significant steps to Viola, still gripping the doorknob. "I'm relieved as well. I think you misunderstood what I meant. It wasn't an improper offer."

"No, of course not," she said. *Do not disagree with the earl,* she told herself. It would be rude. Or silly. Or . . . something, she wasn't precisely sure what, but she didn't want to argue with him now. Not when he was close enough that she could see the faint shadow of whiskers on his jaw and the pulse in his neck and the three different shades of blue in his eyes.

"If I had caused you to lose your position, it would have been my duty to see that you had another," he explained. Almost idly he reached out and took her hand. "But I don't really want to employ you."

"No," she agreed. As if she would get anything done if she saw him every day.

"Do you know why?" His voice was growing softer with each word. His thumb stroked over her knuckles. Viola's knees were softening, and her heart was booming against her ribs.

"I think . . ." She had to wet her lips. "I suspect so."

"Would it be unwelcome to you?"

No. She wanted him to kiss her more than ever, even after she'd just scolded Alexandra for letting a man kiss her, even though she'd been racked with anxiety at the thought of losing her position. Or perhaps that was *why* she wanted him to kiss her, because she'd thought she was on the brink of disaster and had been saved. Because she'd felt on the brink of disaster for most of the house party, and didn't have the will to resist the temptation that was *him* any longer.

For answer she lifted her face to his and leaned forward. Winterton met her halfway, his lips brushing hers like the softest feather. "Winterton," she whispered. "Please—"

"Viola." His hands cupped her jaw. "My name is Wesley. Wes, really."

She smiled in surprise. "Wes?"

"It rhymes with *yes*," he whispered, a laugh lurking in his tone, and then he was kissing her again, not so lightly this time, nor so briefly. Viola moaned when he teased her lips apart and his tongue swept into her mouth. His fingers curled into her hair, loosening the pins until it fell down her back. She arched against him, shivering when her breasts met his chest.

The earl—Wes—made an inarticulate sound of pleasure and gathered her closer. Viola realized she was on her toes, straining against him, clinging to his jacket. She felt drunk with desire, reveling in every shuddering breath he drew, every touch of his hands on her face, her shoulders, her back, her waist. No more was she a mere secretary and he a wealthy earl. In this moment they were simply man and woman, mad for each other.

"Viola." He broke the kiss, his chest heaving. "Viola." He pressed one more hard kiss on her mouth. "God above, I should go."

"I know." She burrowed into his embrace, wrapping her arms around his waist. He was so male and strong and he smelled so good, she had to swallow back an invitation to stay the night here with her. She hoped it was the port making her reckless, but she feared deep down it was far more than that.

"Can I see you again?" His thumb rolled over her lower lip, followed by his own lips in a lingering kiss.

"Every day, my lord," she said breathlessly. "Until you leave."

He went very still. "Can I see you again like this—Viola and Wes, not Winterton and Mrs. Cavendish."

Until you leave, she thought again. "Yes."

A wolfish grin flashed across his face and he kissed her once more, his lips lingering. "God," he moaned. "God help me, I want to stay but I am *going.*"

"Good night," she whispered.

His eyes seemed to glow. "Good night, love."

W es returned to his own room with jaunty steps. What a bloody brilliant idea it had been to come to Kingstag Castle. Thank God Wessex had been away, and was still away. At the moment he didn't even care if the Desnos atlas were here, either. He'd kissed Viola Cavendish, and she had kissed him back. He couldn't wait to do it again.

He tried to check his racing pulse and remind himself to keep his wits about him. She was no society matron, looking for a fleeting affair to amuse herself. She was also not his equal, socially, and she would be cruelly hurt if their attraction to each other caused trouble. The last thing on earth he wanted to do was hurt Viola.

A slight frown crossed his face. How was he to manage this? What would his mother do if a female servant at Winterbury were discovered in an affair with a guest? Of course, Viola was not really a servant, and even servants had some rights to personal relationships. She was the duchess's personal secretary, a position of some importance, independence, and status. What's more, she was a Cavendish cousin, and he . . .

Wes's steps slowed to a halt. She was a respectable woman —not quite a lady but not so far beneath him. He needn't be ashamed of his attraction to her. Why, who knew—in time, he might even—

"What happened?"

The tense question gave him a violent start of surprise. "Good lord, Justin," he snapped. "What do you mean shouting at me?"

His nephew blinked at him in astonishment. He was peering through his barely-opened door. "I didn't shout. You were standing in the corridor staring at nothing. Am I in terrible trouble?"

Right. Justin had been kissing Lady Alexandra. Wes's heart settled into a more normal, if rapid, rhythm. He glanced over his shoulder and motioned for his nephew to let him in. "We'll discuss this privately."

"Well, what happened?" Justin demanded again once Wes was inside and the door was safely closed. "Shall I apologize to the duke? Lady Bridget told me he's not but ten miles away. I could manage it, with a sturdy horse."

"Calm yourself." Wes waved one hand at the chair, but Justin stayed stubbornly on his feet, his hands in fists. Wes shrugged and dropped into the seat himself. "Lady Alexandra has spoken to her mother, who agrees it would be idiocy to make a scandal out of this. I believe Wessex is very protective of his sisters, but with the dowager duchess's support, I don't think you need to fear being called out or marched to the altar."

Justin's face broke with relief. "Thank you, Uncle."

Wes gave him a hard look. "Don't for one moment believe you won't suffer any consequences. Even if Wessex doesn't care a fig for what you did, I care, and so will your mother."

"Mother!" the boy exclaimed. "Why would you tell her?"

"Because this is twice now you've been kissing females without honorable intent." Justin's mouth fell open, and Wes nodded. "I didn't say you had *wicked* intent, but you know perfectly well that if you go around kissing young ladies, you'll find yourself married to one of them before long. Is that what you want?"

"Well—no, not precisely . . ."

Wes rubbed his hands over his face at Justin's cagey tone. "If you think the solution is to kiss maids and tavern wenches, be assured I shall punish you for that. A gentleman doesn't trifle with women, be they noble or ordinary."

His nephew scoffed. "*Some* women—"

"Those are whores," he said bluntly. "Whores are willing because you pay them, not because of your charm and grace, but at least a whore expects nothing but payment from you. Seducing a girl like Lady Alexandra . . ." Wes shook his head. "I couldn't save you from Wessex's wrath in that case—in fact, I'd step up to whip you after he did. You'd do the honorable thing by her, and then spend the rest of your life being a decent husband to her."

Now Justin was offended. "Of course I would! That is, I didn't seduce her—it was only a little kiss—but I am a gentleman and I know my duty—"

Wes rose. "And your desire is to be married before you're twenty-two, before you've had a chance to go to London and meet dozens of pretty girls? Before you've got a chance to travel and see something of the world? Marriage is for the rest of your life, and you've been telling me for days and days that you were so bored in Hampshire you might run mad from it. Now you're ready to become head of the family, bring home a bride, and settle down?"

Justin had flushed progressively redder as Wes spoke. Now he squirmed. "No—not yet, not all that."

"Then mind your behavior. And if you can't, I'll thrash

you until you can. Gentlemen have far more freedom than ladies, and therefore greater responsibility to exercise it wisely. Being young and stupid does not excuse you from the consequences of your actions."

Justin scowled, but wiped it away as Wes raised one brow in warning. "Yes, Uncle."

Wes put one hand on his nephew's shoulder. "We've all been young and stupid, every man one of us," he said in a kinder tone. "It's one thing if you fancy the girl and can see yourself married to her. If you can't . . . you shouldn't be kissing her. Even if you don't get caught by her outraged papa, you give her cruel and misleading ideas about your intentions. You're a cheat and a rogue if you let a girl fall in love with you just so you can steal a few kisses and embraces."

Now thoroughly sobered, Justin nodded. "I understand. I never thought of it that way, but . . . yes, I see."

"Good man." Wes clapped his shoulder. "I don't think you'd like a lady to lead you on, only to refuse you once you were wild for her."

"Not at all." Justin appeared appalled by the thought.

"Then don't do it yourself." Wes let himself out and returned to his own room. Thank God Kingstag was large enough that he and Justin didn't need to share rooms. He needed some peace to think.

The first realization he came to was that he would need to take his own advice, regarding Viola. He did not want her to draw any wrong conclusions from his actions. The second realization, following close on the first, was that he *did* fancy her, more than usual. He liked talking to her. She was sensible and clever and beautiful, and she made him laugh. Wes had no time for idiots or people who were frivolous, and he couldn't recall the last woman he'd looked forward to seeing the way he did Viola.

So what were his intentions?

He pondered the matter as he prepared for bed, and hadn't reached any definite answer by the time he fell asleep. The only thing he knew for certain was that his interest in her was neither shallow nor fleeting. And he yearned to kiss her again.

CHAPTER 9

The next day Viola decided to carry on as if nothing had happened and hope for the best. She'd lain awake until late at night, wondering if she would be called into the dowager's rooms to explain herself, but a summons never came.

Alexandra seemed to have decided the same thing. Every time Viola caught sight of her, she was behaving as she should—well away from Lord Newton. The young viscount, for his part, seemed cowed and quiet as well, and spent most of his time with the other gentlemen.

"Good morning, ma'am." Lord Winterton appeared before her. "May I join you?"

"Good morning, sir. Of course." She had covered a table with evergreen branches and was plaiting them into garlands, an activity that would allow her to monitor the play rehearsal and everyone in it.

Lord Winterton pulled up a chair opposite her. It gave her a splendid view of him, and his lovely mouth that had kissed her so tenderly and magnificently last night. Had that really happened? Covertly she studied him as he poked at the mountain of evergreens on her table. She'd had enough brought in to make a garland that would stretch from here to London and back.

Then he looked up and caught her watching him, and a faint smile touched his lips. Viola flushed warm all over her body. Oh yes, it had really happened. The Earl of Winterton had held her close and kissed her until she could hardly breathe.

He leaned forward. "Viola," he whispered.

Blushing, she also leaned forward. "Yes?"

"I missed you at breakfast," he said, almost inaudibly. "I never realized how much I looked forward to seeing you every morning until you weren't there."

She couldn't stop herself from smiling. "I had work to do." She motioned at the greenery.

"And then? Will you be free to walk out with me and see the sky again? I believe the snow is finally ending."

Viola glanced at the tall windows. The sky was brighter today, but snow still fell. "Perhaps, but I must keep an eye on rehearsal."

"Of course." He picked up a branch and twirled it. "How does one make a garland?"

Her eyes widened in astonishment. "You want to make garlands?"

"I want to sit with you," he said with a searing look. "And I am willing to make garlands to do so."

Oh my. There was a tiny burst of joy in her chest, and her fingers shook as she showed him how to pull apart the branches and twine them around each other to form a long rope. The drawing room was full of people by now, leaving little chance of conversation without being overheard, so they worked in companionable silence. At one point Wes stretched out his legs beneath the table, and Viola lightly rested her slipper on top of his boot. His blue gaze shot to hers, and she almost melted at the hunger in them.

The day flew by. Viola was called away several times to

supervise some aspect of costuming, for the play was to be in a few days. Wes had to go perform his scenes, which sent Viola into gales of silent laughter. A large tea was served midday, and the entire company gathered around the table to consume every crumb of it. Her heart swelled with happiness to see Alexandra laughing and whispering with her friend Kate Lacy, and she felt a rush of relief that Lord Newton seemed more interested in discussing horses with Lord Gosling than in flirting with anyone. All of the guests were in good spirits, and it felt like a sign from above that the party was a success after all.

By the time everyone retired to dress for dinner, Viola had woven a mile or more of garland. She looked at Wes, who was frowning over his much shorter garland, and grinned. "Well done, my lord."

"I haven't done anything worthy of that compliment today, ma'am." He put his hands on the table and half rose from his chair. "Come here."

Viola glanced nervously at the door, but everyone had left. She leaned toward Wes. He closed the distance and brushed his lips against hers. "That's better," he breathed. "Although I might not have done it well enough . . . Let me try again . . ." He kissed her once more, lightly and tenderly, and something inside Viola sang with joy.

Wes sat back, looking pleased with himself. "Much better. I've been waiting all day for that."

Blushing and beaming, she laughed. "Ought you go prepare for dinner?"

He surveyed the greenery piled between them. "I am utterly worn out from all this garland making."

"I hear there is to be dancing after dinner," Viola remarked. "Miss Penworth has agreed to play."

"Dancing!" His face lit. "I feel energized already. Will you dance with me, love?"

Her heart leapt for one wild moment before her brain

reminded her to be cautious. "Perhaps. I must speak to the dowager." He blinked, and she quickly explained. "To let her know how the party is proceeding."

"Is her health improving?"

Viola nodded. "I hope she'll be able to join the guests soon." And take her place as hostess, which would be a vast relief.

He grinned. "I hope so as well. But . . ." He reached for her hand. "You didn't answer my question."

About dancing with him. She hesitated, but the temptation was too great. "Yes."

This time his smile was sensuous and intimate. "That's all I care to know."

They went their separate ways. Viola spoke to the housekeeper about arranging the garland in the hall, then braced herself and went to the dowager's apartment.

It went much better than expected. The dowager was vastly improved, even sitting in a chair by the fire today with a hot brick under her feet. "I have promised Bridget I will attend the play," she told Viola. "Thank heaven I shall be able to."

"I'm very pleased to hear it, ma'am," said Viola fervently.

The dowager smiled. "Has Alexandra kept her word to behave today?"

"Perfectly, Your Grace." She hesitated. "And so has Lord Newton. I believe his uncle spoke to him very strongly about what occurred."

"Very good. Tell me about Lord Winterton."

Caught off guard, Viola jumped. "What?"

"Bridget tells me he fancies you." The dowager's gaze was sharp. "Alexandra says you and the earl discovered her with young Newton, and that she didn't believe that discovery happened because you were searching for her."

Viola could only sit with her mouth open in shock.

The older woman leaned forward. "He's a very eligible

catch, and Sophronia tells me he's not one of those society fribbles. Is he an honest fellow?"

"Y-yes," she stammered.

"Do you, in my daughter's words, 'fancy him'?" Viola couldn't speak. Her answer must have shown on her face, for the dowager sat back. "Remember you are a Cavendish, Viola. Demand that he treat you as such, or Wessex will have his head."

Startled, Viola gaped. "You're—I'm not—That is . . ."

"Am I upset you've caught a gentleman's eye?" The dowager smiled. "No. I know Cleo values you immensely, but you're far too young to spend the rest of your life tending to someone else's family and household. I am not at all surprised, my dear."

"But . . . he is an earl." So far above her.

The dowager's expression softened. "We never know where love may grow. I was the third daughter of a viscount, no one to speak of, and certainly not worthy of a duke. But my dear, I knew it was meant to be the first time Wessex asked me to dance. Do not be afraid to seize happiness when you find it."

"Thank you, Your Grace," she said softly.

Heart soaring, she left. It wasn't quite a mother's blessing, but the dowager's words had been kind and reassuring. It gave her hope. And confidence.

Somehow Wes endured dinner and the blessedly brief round of port among the gentlemen. Every man seemed keen to rejoin the ladies, and when they entered the ballroom Miss Penworth was already seated at the pianoforte.

He tried to disguise his interest in Viola. She sat next to Lady Sophronia, watching as the other guests laughed and danced. Wes asked Lady Alexandra to partner him first, and then Lady Serena. Both were excellent dancers, but he barely registered a moment of it. He was only biding his time.

After two exuberant airs, someone called out to Miss Penworth to play a more sedate country dance so they might catch their breath. Wes seized his chance and approached the settee.

"May I have this dance, ma'am?"

Lady Sophronia's eyes gleamed as she looked him up and down. "If I would grant anyone a dance, it would be you, Winterton. But I haven't danced since Frederick, my fourth fiancé. He was the finest dancer, and spoiled me for every other partner."

Wes grinned and turned to Viola. "I'm sure I could never live up to him. Perhaps Mrs. Cavendish will step out with me, then?"

"Go on, Viola," said Sophronia, wonderful woman. "Dance with the man."

She took his hand, and Wes felt a charge leap up his arm. She gave him a smile, and it was as though the sun had come out. They took their places and he barely remembered what steps to do.

There was no real chance of conversation. Wes was content to gaze at her when they separated. With her dark hair piled up on top of her head and her green eyes alight with happiness, she was entrancing. Every time they clasped hands, her gaze met his, warm and deep and smiling, and he could hardly breathe from how much he wanted her.

When the dance finally ended, he was both relieved and annoyed. Relieved because it ended the torment of watching her without being able to speak to her. Annoyed because now he didn't even have an excuse to watch her. She moved among the guests with quiet grace, suggesting the next dance, helping turn the pages for Miss Penworth, graciously accepting Lord Gosling's invitation to dance. Wes's gaze followed her helplessly around the room, like a smitten boy's.

Everything seemed right when she was around—not only because she had a way of putting everyone at ease, not only because her good cheer never wavered, but because she was the most sensible person Wes had ever met.

After a decade of traveling around the world, Wes had a deep appreciation for people who were able to get things done without fuss or drama. Viola seemed to think of everything and took care of problems before they even happened. The one lapse, Lady Alexandra's stolen kiss with Justin, had happened because he lured her away from the party. Otherwise . . . every arrangement had been pitch perfect. He could tell Lady Serena was somewhat overwhelmed by the demands of being hostess, and Lady Sophronia simply didn't care to mind the details. It was Viola who recognized that Miss Penworth's fingers were growing tired, that Lady Sophronia had nodded once too often, that Lady Bridget was drooping in her chair, and murmured a word in Lady Serena's ear that it was time to end the evening.

Back in his room after everyone had gaily bid the others Happy Christmas and good night—for it was Christmas Eve—he stared into the fire crackling in his hearth, unable to sleep. Was she still working, arranging things for everyone tomorrow? After which she would quietly withdraw into the background, when she deserved to be celebrated as the mastermind of the entire party. Was she enjoying a little sip of port, her mouth rosy and shiny from the wine as she contemplated her work? Had anyone told her how invaluable she was, or how thankful they were she was there?

It was beginning to bother Wes that she was neither hostess nor guest, neither family nor servant, yet everything seemed to rest on her shoulders. Someone ought to thank her, and show appreciation for her unfailing good humor, grace, and charm. Someone ought to make sure she had a happy Christmas, when she had done so much to make it happy for the rest of them.

He wanted her to feel treasured and appreciated. Not only for the way she saw to everyone else's comfort and amusement, but for the way her nose wrinkled when she laughed. For the way she took everything with such good humor and grace. And for the starry look in her eyes when she was well kissed.

He jumped up from the chair and strode to the wardrobe. After a minute of rummaging, he found what he sought. It wasn't much, but he thought she might understand.

His heartbeat seemed to boom in his ears as he made his way through the quiet castle. It was late, nearing midnight. It was almost Christmas Day. When he reached her door, he tapped very lightly and held his breath, waiting.

The first thought through his brain when she opened the door was that her hair was down. It reached below her shoulders, one long curl lying on her breast. Wes's eyes fixed on that curl, on that plump swell of flesh, and his mouth went dry.

The second thought through his brain was that she was in her dressing gown and nightdress.

"Wes," she said softly, and he jerked his eyes up. "What—?"

He cleared his throat. "May I come in?" Her lips parted—damn, how her mouth entranced him. "I have a gift for you," he added.

She blushed the most endearing shade of pink. "Oh no, that's not necessary."

Wes's lips quirked. "Please."

She let him in and closed the door. Without comment he handed her his travel atlas. Viola looked up at him, startled.

"It's not much," he said apologetically. "I've had it with me for years. When I am away from England, it reminds me of home, and when I am in England, it's got splendid maps."

"It's yours? You must keep it—"

"I want you to have it." He shoved his hands into the

pockets of his dressing gown. "It also has descriptions and engravings of scenic vistas all over England and Scotland, so you may see a bit of the world even if you never go beyond Kingstag Castle." He gave a lopsided grin. "Happy Christmas."

Her face went still as she gazed at the book, letting it fall open to an engraving of the cliffs at Dover. Then she looked up at him. There was a lovely flush on her cheekbones, and he could feel her every breath. "Thank you. It's beautiful."

His body roared to life, desire pulsing through him like a tidal wave. Before she could say more he kissed her softly, then harder as her hand went up his chest, around his neck, into his hair.

Every thought fled Viola's brain except the smell and taste and heat of him. Wes pressed her back up against the wall and let his hands roam over her waist, her hips, up to her breasts. She sucked in her breath as his thumb went over her nipple. Wes paused, giving her a searing glance. It was all Viola could do to nod; *yes*, she wanted to say, *more*.

He'd brought her a gift, one of his own atlases. She was still clutching it, the worn leather smooth and soft. Normally she and Stephen exchanged small gifts, or at least a letter, but the snow had kept the mail coach from Kingstag for days. The Duchess of Wessex always gave the staff generous gifts, but Viola knew to expect the same thing the housekeeper would receive. Only Wes had given her something personal, something very dear and valuable to him and therefore wonderful to her. She'd never had her own atlas, nor any need for one. Only Wes looked at her as Viola, who yearned to see the world, not merely the secretary who made everything run smoothly. Only Wes . . .

Looked at her as if she were beautiful and fascinating.

Do not be afraid to seize happiness, echoed the dowager's voice in her head. Viola knew she should be afraid. Not only because he was an earl and she was practically a servant, not only because an affair could cause her to become an unemployed almost-servant, but because Wes could break her heart. Somewhere in the last several days she'd gone and fallen in love with him, with his laughing blue eyes and droll sense of humor and wonderful wicked hands, which were currently exploring her body with exquisite effect.

But instead of choosing the prudent course, she dropped the atlas on the sofa beside her and clung to him, kissing him back with every fiber of her being. Being busy from morning to night as the duchess's secretary hadn't made her forget what it was like to want a man, to be wanted and held and loved by a man.

"Viola," he breathed next to her ear, "I want to make love to you so desperately . . ." His hand cupped her breast, a heady sensation through the soft linen of her dressing gown.

She wasn't afraid. She wanted to seize happiness. Even if just this once, she wanted to feel loved by him. She bit his earlobe gently, making him shudder, and whispered, "Please do."

His hands shook as he unbuttoned her nightgown until it gaped open to her belly. She leaned her head back against the wall, breathing unevenly as he drew the sturdy linen apart, baring her to him. Her pulse felt like a drumbeat between her legs.

"Such beauty," he whispered, his fingers tracing her collarbone. "Such sweetness." His touch drifted lower, swirling over her breast. Viola moaned. "Such passion." He brushed her ribs and Viola quivered. "Viola, I . . ."

She made her eyes focus on him. His hair was wild—from her hands—and his eyes burned as blue as flame. A fine sheen of sweat covered his brow, and he was breathing even harder than she was. "Take off your clothes," she said.

He blinked, and a wicked grin curved his mouth. Without a word he stripped off his dressing gown, his waistcoat, his cravat. He kicked off his shoes and stepped out of his trousers, then pulled the shirt over his head. Viola's throat closed up as he shed his undergarments to stand before her completely nude.

The Earl of Winterton was magnificent, lean and strong and bronzed all over. Only one part of him was untouched by the sun, and her gazed fixed on it. His erection stood straight and thick, and the pulsing between her legs grew stronger.

"May I?" Unabashed at her staring, he fingered the edges of her nightgown. Viola managed to nod, and he slid the garment off her shoulders. "May I?" he whispered again, his hands sliding around her hips. Again she nodded, and he lifted her against him. She put her arms around his neck and hiked her legs around his waist, and he carried her through the open door into her bedroom and rolled them both onto the bed.

He drove her wild with light, teasing touches, then firmer strokes that made her twist and writhe in his arms. He kissed her everywhere, his mouth hot and potent. Viola was the one who finally reached between them and wrapped her hand around his erection. "I want you," she gasped breathlessly. "*Wes.*"

Wes moved over her. His arms bulged as her hand slid up and down his length. Her body humming, Viola guided him between her legs and hooked one leg over his hip. His entire body was taut, and she thought she might burst into flames if he didn't take her then.

He pressed inside, making her gasp. He slid almost out and licked his thumb. "You're so beautiful," he rasped. "I'm about to spend myself just looking at you." He touched her as he slid deep again. Viola arched off the mattress and gripped handfuls of the linens.

Again Wes pulled back. "Open your eyes." His voice had gone ragged. His body was shaking. Viola forced open her eyes and saw that his face was tight with strain. "I want to see the moment when you find your pleasure . . ." He stroked again, his hips moving in slow, hard time with his thumb. Viola stared into his eyes until she couldn't, until the waves of climax made her vision go dark and her body convulsed. She clutched at him and he thrust hard and deep as he kissed her. Dimly she felt him shudder in his own release, but he kept kissing her until she felt soft and exhausted.

"Viola," he murmured as he nuzzled her ear. "I want to stay the night with you."

So he could make love to her again. So she could make love to him, and wake up with his arms around her. Viola gave a sleepy smile. "Please do."

CHAPTER 10

*V*iola had never had a happier Christmas Day.

She woke with Wes stretched out in her bed, looking down at her with a wicked smile. He made love to her again, and only left when the full light of day shone through the small window.

Breakfast was quiet. Withers told her the Cavendish girls had gone to eat with their mother in her apartment, and the other guests were sleeping late. She drank her tea leisurely, wallowing in the memory of every wicked, sensual thing Wes had done.

The rest of the day passed much the same way. Bridget cajoled everyone into one last rehearsal for the play, and dictated several notes for improvement to Viola, but the sun had come out and the young people wanted to go outside. It was cold and bright, and before long the company was throwing snowballs at each other, the ladies shrieking in glee and the gentlemen roaring about battlefield honor and glory. Lord Gosling took a large snowball to the face and Bridget laughed so hard she went head over heels backward into a snowdrift. Lady Alexandra threw one at Lord Newton, who seemed to enjoy it very much. By then Miss Penworth and

Lady Jane had dug a hollow under a tree, and began throwing snow at everyone from the safety of their fort. Viola managed to hit Wes in the shoulder with a snowball, and in retaliation he chased her into the garden, out of sight of everyone, and kissed her among the snow-covered rosebushes.

Tonight Viola was invited to dine with the guests. She wore her best green gown and her mother's pearls, and felt Wes's admiring gaze as if it were a physical touch. When he tapped lightly at her door late that night, she was waiting, ready to spend another night in his arms.

Boxing Day brought a return of duty for Viola. Lady Charlotte Ascot finally arrived, after being snowed in at a roadside inn. The dowager was well enough to come down, swathed in shawls, to present the servants their gifts and thank them. Viola accepted her gifts happily—a length of blue silk, oranges from the hothouse, and five gold guineas—and belatedly sat down to write her brother a letter. She had to share her happiness about Wes with Stephen.

It led to a surprising discovery.

She found Wes in the billiard room with his nephew and some other gentlemen. When he caught sight of her he put down his cue stick and excused himself.

"Come with me." She took his hand. "I want to show you something."

He raised his brows but came with her willingly. Viola led him to the duke's study, quiet and hushed in His Grace's absence. She felt a frisson of nerves just entering the room; normally Mr. Martin came to her when she needed to know something about the duke, to tell the duchess or arrange the calendar. But sometimes she had cause to enter here, as she had earlier today.

"I had to fetch more quills," she said as she closed the door carefully behind them. "Mr. Martin, His Grace's secretary, keeps a supply of the best ones in his desk." She nodded at Mr. Martin's desk in the far corner of the room. "And while I was here, I took the very smallest peek at the shelves. Guess what I discovered?"

Wes's face blanked. "Do you mean—?"

Flushed with eagerness, she nodded. "The Desnos atlas. At least, I believe it is so. It was put away with the other books." She went to the shelves beside Mr. Martin's desk and took out the book she'd seen earlier. "Only you can say for certain." She brought the book to the duke's wide desk and laid it flat.

There was a haunted hunger in Wes's face as he opened the cover. It was not a terribly large book, but it was bound in fine old leather, the titles stamped in gilt. Viola watched his fingers caress the binding, lingering on a small crease near the spine. "It's very like my father's," he murmured. Reverently he opened it, turning a few pages.

"A map of the new world." His finger barely touched the page as he indicated the illustrations. "These were the maps that sent me off to read journals of explorers, and to scalp Anne's doll." He turned another page. "And here—star charts to navigate by! I should have studied these more closely, to be able to discuss them intelligently with you." Viola felt a burst of pleasure at his words. He turned more pages, scrutinizing some in silence and exclaiming over others.

Through it all his enthusiasm for travel shone through. He would pause and relate some story of his travels to India, and to Caribbean islands where pirates roamed. Only when he turned to the end of the book did words fail him. The last two dozen or so pages were covered with close-written notes. Wes's face went still.

"Is it his writing?" Viola ventured.

Silently he nodded, reading.

She slipped her hand into his. It must be bittersweet, to see his father's journal entries in the back of the atlas and know he couldn't have it. This was indeed the atlas the Duke of Wessex had purchased for the duchess.

After several minutes he closed the book, giving the cover one last brush of his hand. "Thank you."

"Perhaps His Grace will be moved by your story," she said.

Wes smiled wryly and shook his head. "I doubt it." He pulled her into his arms. "You found it and gave me a chance to see it again. Thank you."

"I wanted you to see it and know it wasn't lost." She glanced at the atlas in apology. "Even if His Grace won't part with it."

Wes looked at her for a long moment. "You," he said at last, "are extraordinary."

"No," she scoffed. "Very ordinary."

"Not remotely," he whispered, and kissed her. She placed her palms on his chest and went up on her toes, kissing him back. She might not be extraordinary, but *this*—this deep-seated contentment and awe at the way he felt and the way he made her feel—this *love* was the most dazzlingly extraordinary thing she'd ever experienced. Whatever happened later, she would have this moment of true joy and love to remember.

"What the devil?" said a terribly familiar voice. Viola froze, her eyes flying open. Wes raised his head, and as one they turned toward the door.

The Duke of Wessex stood framed in the doorway. As Viola watched, stricken, Mr. Martin peeped around the duke's shoulder before immediately retreating.

Oh dear heavens. She took a step backward and pressed her hands to her burning cheeks. His face as grim as a thundercloud, Wessex strode across the room. "Winterton, I presume."

Wes bowed. "At your serv—"

The duke shoved him backward. "How dare you. Mrs. Cavendish is our cousin."

Wes's eyes flew to Viola, who shook her head mutely. "I meant no offense, sir."

Wessex raised one dark brow. "And yet I find you making love to her in my own private study." Then his gaze fell on the atlas, still on the desk behind them, and his eyes grew dark with anger. "I suppose that is the atlas you wrote to me about."

Wes cleared his throat. "Yes, it happens to be, but—"

"Get out." The duke glared at him.

"Wessex," said Wes, "allow me a moment to explain."

"I see," said the duke with icy finality, "that you have persuaded Mrs. Cavendish to search my personal study to find the book you sought. And I suspect I know how you persuaded her." He looked at Viola for the first time in minutes. "You may go."

Viola wet her lips, but had no words. She never argued with the duke; she barely spoke to him at all. To protest now, when she had violated his trust by invading his study to show her lover one of the duke's private possessions . . . "Sir," she said bravely, "Your Grace . . . If I may . . . It was my fault."

The duke's expression didn't change. "No, ma'am. I wondered at Lord Winterton's persistence in seeking that atlas, but I didn't imagine he would go to this length, corrupting you into helping him."

"Viola? Oh—there are you are." Bridget's bright voice cut through the room. "And Gareth!" With a squeal Bridget launched herself at the duke, who caught her in one arm and kissed the top of her head. "When did you return? Did Helen have the baby? Is everyone well"

"Just now." The duke smiled briefly at his sister. "I'm busy here, and Cleo will be able to tell you all about Helen, who is very well, as is her new daughter."

"How brilliant! A baby girl! And how wonderful you've

come home!" She beamed at him. "We're staging a play tomorrow and now you can see it."

"A play?" Wessex looked at Viola in alarm.

"A farce," Bridget amended. "I wrote it! Everyone is in it except Mama and Aunt Sophronia. It will be the best entertainment at Kingstag in years. I've come to fetch Viola; Lord Gosling is dripping feathers everywhere and no one sews better than she does. Oh, and Lord Winterton must come rehearse his scenes."

Slowly Wessex turned to look at Wes. "He is in your play?"

Bridget nodded. "He plays the king who dies."

The duke's expression darkened. "Very well," he said, still watching Wes. "He'll be down soon. I need a word with him first, Bridget."

"Thank you, Gareth." She bounced up on her toes and kissed his cheek, then hurried out of the room.

"When is the play to be performed?"

"Tomorrow, Your Grace," Viola murmured.

The duke jerked his head. "You may stay until the play is over," he told Wes. "The next morning you leave. I will not have my own cousin's widow seduced under my roof. And if you think to wheedle that atlas from me, I suggest you spare your breath."

Wes's eyes were stormy blue. "If you'll allow me to explain, sir . . ."

"Winterton," said the duke, "I don't care to hear it." This time when he pointed, Viola rushed for the door.

Outside, Geoffrey Martin waited. He was a kind man, and now he simply gave her a sympathetic smile. "Happy Christmas, Mrs. Cavendish."

"Happy Christmas, Mr. Martin," she murmured, feeling as though she would be ill. The duke was not happy. He might be taking it out on Wes at the moment, but eventually he would focus on her part in the debacle. She had escaped being blamed for Alexandra's indiscretion, but she had done even worse.

The study door opened again and Wes stepped out. He nodded once to Mr. Martin, who slipped obediently inside and closed the door again. Wes looked at Viola.

"I must go," she said in a rush. "See to the rehearsal—the costumes—the play is tomorrow, you know—"

He reached for her hand. "I'll speak to Wessex when his temper cools and tell him you weren't to blame."

She backed up, shaking her head. "No. I—I will explain to him. He's been very kind to me so far, and I hope . . . I hope not to lose my position."

A thin line creased his brow. "About your position—"

"No!" She tried to smile, but failed. "I cannot lose my place here, Wes—Lord Winterton. I cannot. The salary is far above what I could expect anywhere else; I told you the duke has been *very* kind. If I lose this position, my brother will have to leave university, and I don't want that. I won't *allow* that." She took another step backward. "Please don't anger the duke further, if you have any care for me at all."

Grim-faced, he gave a faint nod.

Viola blinked back a tear. She had known it wasn't to be forever between them, but she hadn't thought to lose him so soon. Then again, she'd never thought she'd fall in love with him. "Thank you, my lord."

"Viola," he said in a low urgent voice, but she turned and ran, away from his beautiful hands and beguiling laugh and eyes as blue as the midsummer sky.

W es seethed with frustration.

The duke refused to listen to his explanation. Part of him wanted to punch the fellow in the face and make him listen, and part of him knew the duke was absolutely right. If it had been any other fellow kissing Viola in there,

Wes would have thrown that blighter right out into the snow.

The look in her eyes though, when she said she dared not lose her position . . . That look gutted him. She had risked a great deal to show him that atlas, and he was bound and determined that it would not cost her everything.

On the other hand, he didn't like the duke's plan at all. Wessex had told him in no uncertain terms that he was to pack his trunk and be ready to leave early in the morning after the play. It ought to have given him a bit of hope, that the duke was willing to allow him to stay so that Lady Bridget's play wouldn't be spoiled, but all Wes could think of was the second part of the duke's order: never come back.

What are your intentions? echoed his own voice in his head.

He intended to make Viola happy. He intended to win her favor and make her smile at him again. He intended to get her back into his bed, as often as possible. He intended . . . to make her fall in love with him.

What had he told Justin? *If you don't see yourself marrying her, don't kiss the girl.*

He knew that was the answer. Even more, it was the answer he wanted. When he woke in the dawn to see her dark hair spread across the pillow and her beautiful face soft with sleep right in front of him, Wes had known. He would have been content to stay there in that room with her forever, he who had never felt content in one place for more than a few weeks. He had never felt more at home than with her.

Because he was in love. He'd kissed her, he'd fallen in love, and he wanted to marry her.

And that meant he wasn't about to leave without asking her, no matter what the Duke of Wessex said.

The play was going to be an epic disaster.

It began with Miss Penworth declaring that her music had gone missing. Bridget scowled and stomped around until Withers located the pages, under a tea tray in the parlor. Lord Gosling's costume dropped its feathers again, and it took Viola more than two hours to replace them. Everyone else seemed to have forgotten their lines or lost some part of their costume, and two footmen were required to track down people who had wandered off before their scenes. In addition, the Duke of Frye had arrived at last, and no one knew quite what to say to him now. Only Lady Charlotte Ascot seemed willing to speak to him, while Serena had to restrain Bridget from pushing him out into the snow. Blessedly the duchess resumed her role as hostess, both sparing Viola from the job and preventing the duchess from delivering any sort of remonstrance about Lord Winterton.

There was a sharp little pain in her chest every time she thought about Wes, and how he would depart the next morning. She'd lain in bed all night, wishing he could come to her once more and yet terrified that he would. Was it worse to see him as much as possible and lose even more of her heart to him, or to cut herself off now? She didn't know, and ended up stealing longing glances at him across the room as she sewed feathers.

At long last the production was ready to begin. The dowager duchess sat in the audience beside her daughter-in-law and the duke, who wore a wary expression. Sophronia looked filled with eager expectation, which only deepened Viola's sense of impending disaster. Bridget had directed Viola to sit behind the stage with a copy of the script and remind everyone of their lines before they went on. If women could join the army, she reflected, Bridget would be the most fearsome general of them all.

The script had become utterly ridiculous. Viola had Bridget's own copy, which was covered with crossed out sections and additions in the margins. She did her best to keep up, but when Wes approached to make his entrance, dented crown in place, she faltered and busied herself with adjusting Alexandra's ghostly draperies. He strode past her onto the stage. Just hearing his voice made her flinch, and she accidentally stabbed a pin through the draperies into her finger.

When Alexandra went on stage to issue her prophecy about the death of the king, Viola found herself face to face with Wes.

"Do you know your lines, sir?" she asked formally.

He nodded.

"Very good. I'll go where I'm needed, then—"

"Viola!" He caught her hand before she could retreat.

"Please don't," she whispered in distress. It was gouging out her heart to think that he must leave tomorrow morning and she would probably never see him again.

"Just for a moment. Please." She hesitated, undone by the urgency in his face, and he pulled her back behind the curtain at the back of the stage—which had been borrowed from the billiard room.

"The play," she began.

Wes waved one hand as if to shove the play away. "I've just died by decapitation and had my entrails eaten by wolves. I've done my service to Lady Bridget's play. I need to speak to you before Wessex tosses me out."

He wanted to say good-bye. Another wave of misery rolled over her, but she managed a slight nod. She could do this. She had to.

He took a deep breath. "Marry me."

Viola blinked.

"I came here determined to get the Desnos atlas," Wes went on. "I wanted to retrace my father's last journey with it, see what he saw and experience what he did. I've barely spent six months at a time in England since I was eighteen, and I wanted to be off as soon as I recovered the atlas.

"But you said something about travel the other day, that it was no hardship to stay home when everything dear to you was here. When Wessex told me to get out, I didn't even think at all about my father's atlas—all I could think of was that I didn't want to lose *you*. I don't want to go anywhere without you."

"But . . ."

"I love you," he added softly. "If you could care for me enough to give me a chance—"

A sound escaped her, half laugh, half sob. "I fell in love with you when you took me to see the stars."

"Did you?" His face lit up. "Then I have a chance." He pulled her into his arms, his dented crown slipping to one side. "Will you marry me, my darling Viola? Will you travel the world with me and manage my household perfectly when we're home? Will you have a pack of children with me, who will surely vex us almost as much as Justin and Alexandra?"

"Oh, but—but . . ." Viola blushed. "My brother," she said in despair.

"I should be very proud to sponsor his fees," he said. "He can teach me how to navigate."

She smiled, then she laughed, and then she kissed him. "Yes. Yes, Wes, yes."

"You should always say my name that way."

He kissed her again, long and thoroughly. There was an outburst on the other side of the curtain. Viola ignored it for once. The duke and duchess could intervene in any uproar caused by their guests.

"It sounds like Lady Serena has got over being jilted by the Duke of Frye," Wes murmured against her hair.

Viola pressed her cheek to his chest and smiled. "I know."

His laugh rumbled though her. "Did you really?"

She squeezed him tighter. "Since the Christmas Eve rehearsal. She's in love with someone else. I recognize the look."

"Do you?" He tipped up her face to kiss her. "What does it look like?"

She put her hands on the side of his face and smiled, reveling in the way he looked at her. "Like this."

EPILOGUE

ONE YEAR LATER

*W*es woke early, as usual, and reached for his wife, as usual.

*Un*usually, she was not there.

He opened his eyes. The room was quiet and dim, the drapes still closed. The door to the dressing room stood ajar, and no light or sounds came from it, either. Viola must have risen and left some time ago.

Wes flopped back with a stretch and a yawn, and a flicker of disappointment. Tonight was Christmas Eve. Guests had invaded the house, and the only time he had her to himself was here in bed.

One outstretched hand touched paper. There was a note on her pillow, his name on the outside. Intrigued, Wes rolled up onto one elbow and opened it.

No, it was not a note. It was a riddle. His eyebrows climbed as he read Viola's neat script. *Once a wanderer, so at home by sea and saddle, Now confined to hearth and home, must hunger for adventure, To ease the pangs felt with each dawn...*

He re-read the note, a smile slowly forming on his lips. No, it wasn't a riddle.

It was a clue.

"Have a cup of tea," urged Anne, Lady Newton.

Viola hesitated. She'd meant to grab a roll on her way through the dining room, but the whole family had risen early. The children had been allowed downstairs and the table was filled, from infant Maggie in her mother's arms to the dowager Countess of Winterton.

After she and Wes married last Twelfth Night, nearly a year ago, they had come home to Winterbury Hall, where his very curious and amazed family awaited. Fortunately Anne, Wes's oldest sister, had heard an earful from her son Justin, and she was waiting to sweep Viola into an embrace and thank her for dealing so well with Justin's indiscretion.

By summer Viola had become friends with all three of Wes's sisters, Anne, Mary, and Lucy, and found an ally in Margaret, the dowager countess. "I never thought he'd find a woman to make him stay," she'd confided in Viola, "and I'm unutterably pleased it was you, dear."

And now they were all at Winterbury Hall for Christmas, like a proper family. It filled Viola with happiness. The only flaw was the absence of her brother Stephen, but she could not hold it against him. Wes had helped Stephen secure a chance to study telescopes in Brussels, to Stephen's delirious joy. Ah well. She was glad he was getting to do what he loved so dearly. He had promised to visit when he returned.

"Yes, do sit down," added Margaret.

"You've been racing about this entire week, you deserve a proper breakfast at least," put in Lucy from the end of the table.

Viola put a hand on the empty chair. Hot tea sounded divine, but… "I still have so much to do."

"I'll watch out for Uncle Winterton," offered Justin, divining what made her hesitate. Viola gave the young man a grateful smile, and he grinned back. He jumped up from his chair and loped to the door, followed by his young cousin Tom, quietly begging to be allowed to keep watch, too.

As Viola slid into the chair, the other ladies sprang into action. "Freddie, bring her some toast," Lucy told her husband. Mr. McPherson obediently went to the sideboard while Anne poured a steaming cup of tea and Grace, her youngest daughter, passed the milk and honey.

"Thank you all." Viola took a sip, her eyes flickering closed in pleasure. "I must hurry, though."

"You must also eat," said Margaret firmly. "Catherine, dear, pass the butter."

"And the strawberry jam." Catherine gave Viola a jaunty smile as she slid the butter and jam across the table. Viola grinned back; she and Anne's second daughter both loved their butter and jam.

"Is all ready?"

"Nearly," replied Viola buttering her toast. "Thanks to Freddie and Sir Thomas."

Freddie McPherson and Sir Thomas Steventon both protested, but Viola insisted. "I could not have done it without your help—*everyone's* help," she added, looking around the table.

"It was our pleasure, my dear," Margaret assured her.

"And the least we could do." Mary shifted three-year-old Mary Anne from her lap to the chair beside her, and gave Viola an affectionate glance. "After you invited us all for Christmas."

A chorus of "Thank you, Aunt Viola!" sounded around the table from the younger family members. Sir Thomas raised his coffee cup in salute, and Freddie winked at her. Both Wes's brothers-in-law had been invaluable, but even the children had been willing conspirators, once she explained what she wanted to do.

"Uncle will be so astonished!" Jane, Anne's eldest daughter, bounced in her chair with glee, acting more like a child than a young lady on the verge of making her debut.

"Only if we all keep the secret," piped up her cousin George.

Freddie ruffled his son's hair. "Which we shall, eh, lad?"

"Of course we shall!" he answered stoutly. "It's a great lark. All the fellows at school will be amazed that Aunt Viola pulled off such a prime prank." George had just finished his first term at Eton.

"'Tis not a prank," scolded Catherine. "'Tis a gift."

"*And* a surprise," chirped her sister Grace. "The best kind of surprise!"

From the hall came the sound of the clock, chiming the hour. "Of goodness, I must hurry!" Viola drained her tea cup. "Wes is such an early riser."

"He always has been!" Margaret shook her head. "The trouble that boy got up to, rising before anyone else in the house..."

"Did he?" demanded George, interested. "Tell, tell, Granny!"

Viola smiled at the chatter as she took her last bite of toast and rose from the table. "He's coming!" yelped Justin from his place at the door. "He's descending the stairs!"

Viola seized her notebook and dashed for the opposite door, which young Tom sprinted to open. Silver and china clattered as everyone resumed eating, and she just heard Justin say, "Good morning, Uncle!" as the door closed behind her.

• • •

Wes had become accustomed to finding *someone* at breakfast—the house was full of people these days—but he also usually found find Viola.

Today he found his entire family. A dozen faces looked up at him and cried, "Good morning!"

He paused warily. Not only his mother but all three sisters, both brothers-in-law, and their children. "Good morning."

"Come in!" His mother beckoned him. "Such a lazy one you are this morning!"

Wes started. He, lazy? The clock had chimed eight as he came downstairs. "I didn't think to see you waiting for me this morning."

A burst of laughter greeted this. "Waiting!" cried his mother. "How silly. We were just hungry. Cook has made poached eggs, your favorite."

He looked at her strangely. He'd never liked poached eggs.

"There's rashers of bacon, too," piped up his nephew George. "Good and hot, too, not cold like at school."

"And butter buns!" added his niece Grace.

"Buns!" crowed little Mary Anne, waving her hands so hard, the bun she held flew right across the table, where her father Sir Thomas neatly caught it.

"Excellent," said Wes after a moment. He went to the sideboard and filled a plate, his brain working furiously. Why were they all here? So early? And where was Viola?

He took his plate to the head of the table. "Has anyone seen Viola?"

"No, not at all!"

"Viola? I've no idea."

"Not this morning, Uncle."

"Would you like some coffee?"

Wes stared in amazement at Justin, who advanced on him

with the coffee pot. He glanced around the table. "What's going on?"

"Nothing! Coffee?" Justin lifted the pot aggressively. Mary Anne let out a giggle and clapped her hands over her mouth when Mary shushed her.

"And no one has seen Viola at all today?"

"Not a glimpse," said Margaret calmly. "Were we supposed to keep an eye on her?"

Wes frowned and stabbed at his bacon. "No. It's just odd that she's not here."

"She must be extremely busy," said Anne. "Preparing for Christmas."

"She's done so much," added Mary. "You must be prepared to make allowances, when guests are in the house."

"Such a wonderful party it is, though, Uncle," gushed Catherine.

"She's an angel to have us all here for Christmas, you do know that, don't you, Wesley?" That was Lucy, bouncing baby Maggie in her arms.

"I do." But he was less and less pleased about it. Moodily he ate as his family chattered about neighborhood gossip. If it were such a lot of work, surely Viola should have break-fast, shouldn't she? "Was she here earlier?" he asked abruptly.

His mother blinked at him. "Who, dear? The vicar and his wife? They've gone into Derbyshire to see their daughter."

"Viola," he said through his teeth. "Has anyone seen her this morning?"

A strangely fraught hush fell. "I believe I saw her walking in the garden," said Justin at last, his eyes flicking from his mother to his grandmother.

"Are you certain? I'm sure I saw her heading toward the kitchens," said Lucy.

"No, she must be with the housekeeper. She did hint there would be a splendid dinner tonight." Anne wagged her finger at him. "Be patient, Winterton! You cannot keep her in your pocket all the time."

I don't want her in my pocket, Wed groused to himself. *I only wanted her in my arms for a morning kiss.*

He shoved back his chair. "All right. I shall see you at dinner."

"But where are you going?" protested his mother. "We were hoping to…"

"Play charades!" cried Grace as her voice trailed off. "Please say you will, Uncle!"

Wes's eyes flitted around the table again, suspiciously. Something was definitely up. "Perhaps later."

"I nearly forgot," said his mother hastily. "Viola did ask me to give you this."

Wes all but snatched the note from her hand. With no great surprise he saw it was another riddle.

Far from the foreign bazaar, a league removed from thrills, A man must simpler pleasures apprehend, A stroll, a quiet vista, the written page, There lie adventures large and small without end…

He headed for the library.

"**I**s that everything?"

Mr. Jenkins, the stable master, nodded. "Aye, m'lady."

Excellent. Viola surveyed the boxes they'd brought. Anne and Lucy were planning to come help her unpack them.

"Thank you." She smiled and nodded at Billy and Johnny, the grooms who had finished unloading the wagon. "Go on and take the rest of the day free. No one will go out today."

They thanked her and piled back into the wagon, rattling back up the newly widened path toward the stables. Humming softly, Viola took the broom and finished sweeping the floor. She could have sent the maids out to do this—all of it—but felt it meant a little more if she did it herself. She was still getting used to being in charge of a whole household, and she'd asked a great deal of all the servants by inviting so many guests.

But that, she did not regret. Wes had raised his brows, but she'd seen him walking the grounds with Justin, explaining why he'd done something or other around the estate. She'd heard him laughing and jesting with his sisters, who teased him with the affection of older siblings. He'd gone shooting and riding with Freddie and Thomas, and promised trips to London to his nieces, and playing bowls with the little ones. For all his wandering, he loved his family. And they were beyond delighted to have him home.

She pinned a large map of the world on the wall and put fresh candles in the sconces beside it. She paused to study it. Wes had suggested any number of places where they might go on a wedding trip, but Winterbury Hall had been neglected; they were needed here. He'd promised her it was only postponed, but now it would be months before they could go.

Her eyes lingered on Brussels. "Happy Christmas, Stephen," she whispered, pressing a kiss to her fingertip and touching it to that spot on the map. "Next year."

She was putting sprigs of evergreen in the windowsills when Anne and Lucy arrived. Lucy flung herself out of the gig and raced to the door. "Disaster!"

Viola jerked upright, her heart pounding. "What?"

Anne hurried up beside her. "Not disaster," she said with a stern look at her sister. "But... not good news. Winterton has left, and no one knows where he's gone or when he will return."

W es found the clue Viola had left in the library—*Every journey begins and ends at home, And every traveler must know the way. The best guide one could find, Is a loyal steed in want of hay*—and was on his way to the stables. He had no idea what she was up to, but he was more and more amused and intrigued by it. His curiosity had reached unbearable levels, and he'd begun wondering if—or rather, *hoping*—he would find her at the end, reposing in a steaming bath with her hair up and that beguiling twinkle in her eye, ready to wish him a very happy Christmas in private. It was, after all, the one year anniversary of the first time he'd made love to her...

Unfortunately Rivers, the butler, intercepted him. "Mr. Gardnew has returned, my lord."

Wes stopped. "Where?"

"The morning room, sir."

He was already on his way, his heart leaping. He'd given up hope, but now there was a chance. He flung open the door, almost holding his breath. "Well?"

"Put into Eastbourne this morning, my lord," replied Gardner, his face red from cold. "The weather cleared as if by divine will."

Wes couldn't keep back a grin of fierce elation. Inside he was shouting with it. "Excellent news, Mr. Gardner! Via the Pevensey road?"

"Yes."

He changed his mind about finding Viola. He'd not thought this surprise, the gift she wanted above all else, would arrive in time. He was sure she would like the emerald parure wrapped in silver tissue hidden in his study, but this... *this* would please her far more. "I'll ride out at once."

"Will you, sir?" asked his steward in surprise. "It's not necessary. I made all the arrangements..."

"I know, and I've every confidence they are excellent. I simply want to make certain there's no delay."

"Shall I come with you?"

Wes smiled. "If you wish, but feel free to stay and warm yourself with a cup of mulled wine. I appreciate all your efforts and cannot ask more of you."

Gardner gave a rueful grin. "I've seen it this far, might as well finish it. Let me get a fresh horse."

Wes clapped his shoulder. "I cannot believe we've pulled this off."

Gardner laughed as they headed for the stables. "Nor can I! 'Tis a Christmas miracle, indeed!"

V iola had rearranged the ivy and pine boughs, trimmed the candle wicks, and straightened every pillow. The winter light was fading, and she'd sent Anne and Lucy back to the house with the gig. She was wasting time and she knew it.

Whatever had sent Wes haring off—and no one at the house seemed to have the slightest idea what it was—he hadn't returned. The butler had sent word that Mr. Gardner, the estate steward, had ridden up in a lather, and then both of them had taken off. That suggested an emergency somewhere on the estate, which of course he must see to at once.

She told herself her disappointment was her own fault. If she'd just told Wes this morning, instead of leaving little clues to send him on a treasure hunt, he would have come right down. They could have had breakfast together before he was called away. Now she had spent most of the day waiting for him, and it was growing dark.

Ah well. It was a small disappointment, after all. Smiling wryly at herself for moping over it, she went to put out the lamps and return to the house. Tomorrow morning she would tell him, first thing.

"I say, this charming cottage has a very fetching lady in it," said his voice behind her, warm with amusement.

Viola whirled. "Wes!"

He opened his arms and she flew to him for a long kiss. "I've been waiting all day for that," he breathed, holding her close.

She smiled up at him. "I should have stayed in bed this morning, shouldn't I?"

"With me? Always," he replied, making her blush and laugh. "But what are you doing here?"

'Here' was the small former gamekeeper's cottage at the edge of the woods, facing the largest pond on the estate. She stepped back and spread her arms. "I know how much you wish to travel and see the world, and get away from the cares of Winterbury. I cannot offer you Sicily or St. Petersburg, but I hope this will be a peaceful retreat from the estate."

His face had gone blank with astonishment. He looked around the cozy little cottage. Freddie and Tom had overseen the renovation, removing some of the walls that cut it into three tiny rooms and made it one large room. It was still rustic, with comfortable but simple furnishings and walls washed white, and thick warm drapes covering the windows that overlooked the pond. Bookcases framed the stone hearth, where the fire was burning low, and a pair of deep wingback chairs sat in front it, inviting a relaxed cup of tea or a class of brandy over a good book.

And the map. It covered an entire wall, richly illustrated and detailed. Wes caught sight of it and crossed the room slowly, entranced.

"You created this for me," he said softly, his fingers tracing the frothing wake of a sailing ship at sea. "With sea monsters," he added with a sudden laugh, spying the gilled serpent lurking in the depths of one ocean.

"What decent map doesn't?" She put her arms around his waist.

He kissed the top of her head. "Thank you, my love. I hope you don't regret it when I hide from Anne and Justin here."

Viola smiled and stepped out of his embrace. "And now I can give you your gift!"

"Now!" He laughed in surprise. "As if I haven't got every-thing I want…"

She retrieved a parcel wrapped in linen and handed it to him with a shy smile. "Happy Christmas, my love."

Lips quirked, he undid the folds, and then his mouth dropped open and he simply stared.

"Are you pleased?" she asked, a bit anxiously.

He raised stunned eyes to her. "How did you get this?"

It was the Desnos atlas he'd gone to Dorset in search of a year ago, the object that took him to Kingstag Castle and into her life. But a year ago, it had belonged to the Duke of Wessex, intended as a gift for his wife the duchess. The duke had utterly refused to sell it.

"Her Grace sent it to me," she explained. "She read your father's writings in the back and realized how much it must mean to you. She said she could not keep such a dear memento of someone so beloved, and sent it with cordial wishes."

His face was very still as he paged through the atlas. "I never thought I would see it again. To tell the truth, I'd made peace with that. These days my mind is more agreeably occu-pied, with my deeply beloved wife."

She blushed. "Now you have both."

"Viola." He laid the atlas on the table between the armchairs. "Having my father's journal restored to me is astonishing and marvelous beyond words. Thank you." She beamed at him. "Now, does this cottage contain a bed?"

"A chaise longue." She arched one brow. "Are you in need of a respite?"

"No," he murmured, "I wish to thank you properly for the atlas." He bore her backwards onto that chaise with a growl, until her giggles turned into breathless sighs of delight.

•   •   •

Some time later, Wes lay sprawled on the chaise feeling at perfect charity with the world. The cottage did feel like a private little world, simple and far removed from the responsibility of Winterbury Hall. *A respite,* she'd called it. Yes, that was ideal, he thought, pressing his lips to her forehead as she snuggled against him.

"If I might suggest one small improvement," he murmured, "perhaps a larger chaise."

Viola laughed. Her hair tumbled around her shoulders in fetching disarray, and she only wore her shift. "Perhaps."

His fingers played with her loose hair. He loved undoing her, laces and buttons and hairpins. "I suppose now I should give you your gift."

She kissed his jaw. "I think you just did."

"That!" He grinned. "That was my everyday expression of love and appreciation. I've got something special for you."

Viola propped her chin on his chest and smiled dreamily at him. "Never say *that* wasn't special."

He laughed. "It was extraordinary! However"—he kissed her on the mouth—"there's something else waiting at the house. Shall we go see?"

Surprise flickered over her face, but she sat up and reached for her gown. Wes kissed his way up her back as he did the buttons, making her laugh. After banking the fire and donning hats and cloaks against the twilight chill, they closed the cottage door and headed back to the house, hand in hand.

At the Hall he handed their cloaks to the butler and urged Viola toward the large drawing room, from which came the sounds of conversation and laughter. "Let me go change," she whispered, resisting.

"You look beautiful."

"My hair is a dreadful tangle, Wes…"

He wiggled his eyebrows at her. "And it looks ravishing that way."

She tried to look stern, but was smiling when he led her into the brightly lit room.

The cousins were playing charades. His mother and sisters sat on the sofas, watching and laughing at the children's antics. Freddie and Tom stood near the punch bowl by the window, and with them—

"Stephen!" cried Viola. "Oh, Stephen, you're *here*!" She ran across the room and flung herself into the arms of her tall, lanky brother, just arrived from Brussels via Eastbourne and then Pevensey.

Wes watched fondly as his wife and her brother put their heads together, their hair the same shade of chestnut. When she turned and flew back to him, her eyes glowing and her face shining with joy, he caught her to him. "If you brought my family to me, I should bring your family to you," he whispered in her ear. "Happy Christmas, darling."

She took her face in his hands. "This is the happiest Christmas I've ever known." And she kissed him, and he kissed her, and neither cared that everyone in the room was watching and smiling, too.

AFTERWORD

Map of a Lady's Heart was originally published as part of the anthology **At the Christmas Wedding**, featuring wonderful stories by Maya Rodale and Katharine Ashe. If you want to read more about how the Mr. Gray, inland pirate of Shropshire, won Lady Serena's heart, and why the Duke of Frye jilted Serena so coldly and cruelly—or perhaps not so cruelly—**At the Christmas Wedding** is available from online retailers, in ebook, print, and audio.

And don't miss the prequel to this story, also set at Kingstag Castle: **At the Duke's Wedding**, featuring many familiar faces, especially Lady Sophronia.

A Rake's Guide to Seduction

Other Novels

What a Woman Needs

Novellas and Collections

When I Met My Duchess in At the Duke's Wedding

Map of a Lady's Heart in At the Christmas Wedding

A Fashionable Affair in Dressed to Kiss

Will You Be My Wi-Fi? in At the Billionaire's Wedding

Short Stories

A Kiss for Christmas

Like None Other

Written in My Heart

ABOUT THE AUTHOR

Caroline Linden was born a reader, not a writer. She earned a math degree from Harvard University and wrote computer software before turning to writing fiction. Since then the Boston Red Sox have won the World Series four times, which is not related but still worth mentioning. Her books have been translated into seventeen languages, and have won the NEC Reader's Choice Award, the Daphne du Maurier Award, and RWA's RITA Award.

Visit www.CarolineLinden.com for excerpts, bonus features, and to subscribe to her news.